Mother's hand shot to her mouth, and she shook her head. "No, no, no!"

Bit by bit, Father pulled every last detail from Josiah. How Solomon had engaged the British sentry, how Josiah had killed him. How he had spent the night at the fort and fought with the Green Mountain Boys, and how Mr. Reid had also died.

"These Patriots and their illusions of independence. It's evil, that's what it is." Father slammed his fist into the table hard enough to send a splinter into his hand. "And now we're the ones suffering for it. At least you had the good sense to come home." He leaned toward his remaining son. "I tell you this much. I know you have a soft spot for the Reid girl. But don't you dare think of helping them out. Or any of those traitors to the king. I had urged moderation in the treatment of those wretched Patriots, but not anymore."

Confusion must have shown on Josiah's face, because Father continued, shouting now. "I won't be satisfied until we chase every one of them off their land and get it back for King George. Including those Reids. And if you set one foot in an enemy's house—don't bother coming home."

After Solomon's death, Josiah would do almost anything his father asked.

Except neglect Sally Reid.

Award-winning author and speaker **DARLENE FRANKLIN** recently returned to cowboy country—Oklahoma—to be near family. She loves music, needlework, reading, and reality TV. She has published six books previously, with many more on the way. This fall she is celebrating the repacking of her Rhode Island romance in Seaside Romance and her third novella anthology, *Face of Mary in A Woodland Christmas*. Visit Darlene's blogs at www.darlenefranklinwrites.blogspot.com and thebookdoctorbd.blogspot.com.

Books by Darlene Franklin

HEARTSONG PRESENTS
HP650—Romanian Rhapsody
HP855—Beacon of Love

The Prodigal Patriot

Darlene Franklin

Heartsong Presents

To the granddaughters of my heart, Savannah and Shannon
O'Hara. You captured my heart the first time I met you; I'm
so glad God brought our lives together.

A note from the Author:
*I love to hear from my readers! You may correspond with
me by writing:*

Darlene Franklin
Author Relations
PO Box 721
Uhrichsville, OH 44683

ISBN 978-1-60260-904-4

THE PRODIGAL PATRIOT

All scripture quotations are taken from the King James Version of the
Bible.

All of the characters and events in this book are fictitious. Any
resemblance to actual persons, living or dead, or to actual events is
purely coincidental.

*Our mission is to publish and distribute inspirational products offering
exceptional value and biblical encouragement to the masses.*

PRINTED IN THE U.S.A.

one

Maple Notch, Vermont
May 1777

Today was a glorious day to be outside, Sally Reid decided as she went about her morning chores. Cool air flowed down from the mountains, scented with pine, the evergreen trees that gave the "Verts Monts," or the Green Mountains, their name. The sun overhead promised sunshine and warmth, and green shoots pushed up through the ground. She loved the rhythms of farm life, the cycles of sowing, growing, reaping, and resting. A song of praise burst from her lips.

"Good morning, Miss Reid! You sound cheerful this fine morning," a deep voice called out.

Sally stopped in mid-verse. Her singing called for no audience beyond the chickens who clucked along with her. Pa teased that she had the voice of a crow. Of all people, who should catch her in her morning serenade but Josiah Tuttle.

"Morning to you, Mr. Tuttle."

He smiled at her, the same grin that had infuriated her since childhood. It always put her in mind of the day he pulled the mobcap off her head after she'd had the measles. Clumps of her straight, oak-colored hair came off with the mobcap, and she had run home and refused to come out again. Remembering, she put a hand to the top of her head, making sure its covering was in place.

Josiah's hair was as black now as it had been then, the same red highlights created by the sun. But the years had transformed him from a skinny lad to a stalwart man, tall and well built. Not that she would ever make mention of the fact.

"Is Nathaniel about yet?" His voice had changed as well, into a marvelous baritone. He could sing far better than she could.

"I haven't seen him." Sally wondered if they required a chaperone for this conversation. Anyone could see them in the open dooryard. In fact, she saw a flicker in the opening in the cabin wall—probably her little sister, Nellie. Next thing Sally knew, Nellie would start announcing that Josiah was calling on her to everyone who stopped by.

The cabin door opened, and her brother Nathaniel came out. "Mornin', Josiah. Are you ready?"

Sally looked from one to the other. "What are the two of you planning?"

"Sorry I'm late." A younger version of Josiah ran into the clearing, his brother, Solomon. From a distance they looked much alike, both of a height, with dark hair and an easy gait. Up close, the resemblance was even more startling, the same high, broad foreheads and thin noses so like their father's.

"Where are all three of you going?" Solomon's arrival had piqued Sally's curiosity.

"Don't you remember what day it is?" Nathaniel seemed offended that she should ask.

"Of course I do. It's May 11."

"And two years ago today, Ethan Allen claimed Fort Ticonderoga 'in the name of the Great Jehovah and the Continental Congress.'"

"So you're off to celebrate the Revolution?" The word rolled off Sally's tongue. Her family supported independence—especially the Green Mountains' independence. With both New Hampshire and New York squabbling over who could lay claim to their land, Vermont had declared itself an independent country: the Republic of New Connecticut or the Republic of the Green Mountains. "Are you going off to win the war, then?" She doubted it. Pa would have alerted the family if the Green Mountain Boys were gathering.

"The war isn't a joke." Solomon used his most serious tone. He must have sensed her hesitation. Of the three young men, he took his responsibilities with the militia the most seriously. When Mr. Tuttle forbad his sons to take part in the glorious victory at Fort Ticonderoga, Solomon had almost gone in spite of his father's stricture against joining the Patriot cause.

Sally sobered. "Of course not."

"Some of us are gathering over by Whitson's farm to celebrate. Maybe drill a little." Nathaniel would gladly pitch his chores for an opportunity to do battle against the hated British. He liked drilling a lot more than farming.

"Does Pa know?" Sally didn't want to get into trouble if Nathaniel disappeared.

"I reminded him last night." Nathaniel grinned at her. "We'd best be going, or we'll miss the others." He and Solomon turned as one and raced toward the trees crowding the edge of the field.

Josiah stayed behind long enough to pull the front of his tricorne over his dark eyes. "I'll be seeing you, Miss Reid."

That man. How could he bother her so and leave her smiling at the same time?

❧

Josiah whistled a happy song as he walked away from the Reid cabin, his face probably reflecting a silly expression. Women. He'd never understand them, Sally Reid in particular. When he saw her tug at her mobcap today, he knew she was thinking about that incident all those years ago. Would she ever forgive him for that boyish trick? Their little school had closed down, with so many out sick, and then the funerals started. They had buried his only sister during that awful time. His whistle faltered and stopped. Then he started up again. That was all a long time ago, and God had spared him and Sally, as well as many others.

He soon caught up to Solomon and Nathaniel. His brother took one look at Josiah and opened his mouth, a grin on his face.

Josiah glared at him, and Solomon shut his mouth. Wise man.

"What are your intentions toward my sister?" Nathaniel asked.

"If I have any intentions—and I repeat, *if*—I won't be telling you." Josiah wouldn't let Sally's brother rile him that easily.

A smirk formed on Nathaniel's face.

"Wipe that grin off your face. I'm still older and bigger than you."

"Yes, sir." Nathaniel straightened his lips with apparent difficulty and changed the subject. "What do you think we'll do today?"

Josiah didn't know. If this ran along the same lines as last month's celebration of the beginning of the Revolution at Lexington and Concord, young Whitson would bring corn whiskey. Add everyone's musket to the mix, and Josiah didn't care for the result. As his father said, whiskey and firepower didn't go well together. At least they both agreed about that one thing. If only Father could see the importance of fighting for the rights of the colonies and not see them as toys to be played with at King George's leisure.

Once again, he found himself lagging behind Nathaniel and Solomon. He spent too much time thinking about Sally. Given a choice of a morning teasing Sally or a morning listening to young men who should know better drinking whiskey and talking brave talk, he knew what he'd choose. He prayed he could be a voice of reason and override Whitson's wildness.

Whitson's farm lay at the far end of the valley between two mountains where Maple Notch nestled. By the time they neared it, the sun had risen high overhead. Loud laughter reached his ears, suggesting the keg had already made a couple of rounds. *Too late.*

He stopped in midstride. "Solomon."

His brother looked at him, annoyed. "Why are you stopping? We're almost there."

Josiah put a hand to his arm. "Promise me you'll keep your head."

Solomon shook him off. "I never go off at half cock, and you know it."

Because Father never lets it get that far. Once again, Josiah wondered if they had made a mistake in going. God help him, he wanted to be here as much as Solomon did.

A branch broke ahead of them, and Whitson stumbled into their path. "Welcome! We wondered if you would make it." He wasn't drunk, not really. Something other than whiskey had excited him. "We found ourselves a bit of fun to celebrate our independence."

Loud grunts like someone in pain reached Josiah's ears.

Had a Redcoat found his way to Maple Notch? Was an army on the way? The distressed sound gave speed to Josiah's feet, and he sprinted to the clearing.

A man dressed in ordinary civilian clothes knelt on a waistcoat on the ground. His blood dripped from stripes across his back and stained the silk lining. The man's hair hung around his face, hiding his features. Ordinary breeches ended just below the knee. This man was no soldier. A spy?

A compass, telescope, quill, and paper lay strewn across the ground—the equipment of a surveyor.

"What are you doing?" The sound of his own voice startled Josiah. He hadn't meant to speak aloud.

"Please, sir, I beg of you, I am no lover of the British. I am here on behalf of the state of New York."

Josiah knew the man's origin as soon as he spoke. His broad accent marked him as a flatlander, not a Vermonter born and bred.

"I mean no harm." The man raised his head, and Josiah looked into clear blue eyes that pled for mercy but expected none. Josiah had little enough love for New York's attitude toward the Green Mountain region, but this was unconscionable.

"He's plotting *our* valley to give away to those New Yorkers." Young Linus held a rod between his hands.

"I say, let 'em try," said one of the men, drunker than the rest.

"We'll send this man back as our emissary." Whitson sounded like a schoolmaster instructing his students. "He can tell them what kind of reception to expect if they show up here."

Anger boiled inside Josiah. "Solomon? Nathaniel?"

The three of them formed a thin line between the surveyor and the celebrating militiamen.

"You've had your fun for the day. The Green Mountain Boys are better than this. You'd better hope Mr. Allen doesn't get word of what you did here." Josiah glanced at the man on the ground. "May I have the honor of your name, sir?"

"It's Van Dyke. Schyler Van Dyke."

"Mr. Van Dyke. Are you able to stand?"

In answer, he pushed up on one leg and lurched forward. Solomon draped one of the man's arms over his left shoulder, keeping his musket ready in his right, and helped him to his feet. With him standing, the extent of the man's injuries became more visible. One eye was already swelling shut; blood coated his nose, and his right arm hung limply by his side. He needed immediate care. Josiah knew he should leave without speaking further, but he couldn't stop himself.

"I'm sure you consider yourselves great Patriots, attacking an innocent civilian. An American, no less." He snorted. "Next time, save your bravery for when you see the Redcoats coming."

Nathaniel put an arm around Van Dyke's chest, avoiding the broken arm, and the three men walked toward the path home. Josiah lingered, walking backward, musket ready in his hands if someone interfered.

"At least my father's not a Tory." Whitson threw one last barb as the quartet approached the edge of the forest.

Behind Josiah, he felt Solomon stiffen at the insult.

"Peace," he whispered. "Now's not the time."

"My. . .supplies," Van Dyke managed to gasp. "All my maps. . ."

Solomon shook his head, but Josiah sensed how important they were to the man. "We'll get them later if we can. But I'm afraid they're lost to you. Be thankful you have your life."

Branches closed behind them as they entered the forest, and Josiah turned to avoid stumbling over unseen obstacles.

"Are you Tories, then?" Van Dyke panted through the words. "If you are, you keep strange company, showing up at a gathering of the local militia."

Josiah glanced at Solomon. Consternation twisted his face. With Patriotic fervor sweeping the colonies, the issue of Tory against Patriot divided more than mother country and colony. It sundered towns and even families. Josiah didn't answer.

Nathaniel jumped in when Josiah didn't reply. "These two aren't. They're good Vermont boys. But their father believes differently." He gave an apologetic shrug.

A sheen of sweat broke out on Van Dyke's brow. Josiah judged they had traveled far enough to afford a stop. "Let's tarry here a minute." He led the injured man to a large rock and handed him a skin of water.

The man's hands trembled as he lifted it to his lips, and some spilled to the ground before he managed to gulp down several mouthfuls. "It wouldn't matter to me if you were. I do my job and try stay out of trouble." He grimaced and lost some of the water. "Most of the time I succeed, but not today." He handed the skin back to Josiah. "Where are you taking me? To gaol?"

A bubble of laughter escaped Josiah's lips at that. "The last I knew, surveying land wasn't a criminal offense. But you've raised a good question."

"We'll take him in." Nathaniel offered. "I'm sure Ma won't mind."

Josiah's heart quickened. "That sounds wise. Mrs. Reid has a healing hand." More than that, he would have an excuse to stop by and talk with Sally when he checked on Van Dyke.

"But are you sure? I understand she's been feeling poorly."

"Ma would skin me alive if she found out I'd refused an opportunity to practice hospitality. She'd say Mr. Van Dyke here might be an angel unawares. She'll take care of anybody—even a Tory." Nathaniel flashed a grin so like his sister's that Josiah had to smile back.

"I don't want to bring trouble on anyone," Van Dyke protested. "If you could take me to the nearest inn, I'll be on my way."

"You couldn't make it there today." The man might not even manage the trip across the valley. "In the morning, we'll see."

The trip back took longer than the morning run, with frequent stops for Van Dyke's sake. During one of the rest periods, Nathaniel carved a strip from a willow tree. Josiah nodded his approval. Willow bark tea might help reduce any fever and pain.

The sun had passed the zenith by the time they reached the Reids' farm. Mr. Reid worked his way down a row, plucking small fish out of a bucket and dropping one on each mound as he went.

"Hallo!" Josiah called out in greeting.

Mr. Reid straightened his back, put a hand to his eyes to block the sun, and peered in their direction. "Nathaniel! Josiah, Solomon! I thought you had gone to celebrate the capture of Fort Ticonderoga. What happened?" He set down the bucket of fish and trotted through the field.

At least Mr. Reid knew why the local lads had gathered. Nathaniel needed no subterfuge.

"Whitson." Nathaniel spit out the *s* in the name.

"I'm a surveyor from New York," Van Dyke explained.

"Some of the local boys took exception to my occupation."

"You need say no more." A scowl darkened Reid's face, whether because of New York's interference or the treatment the man had received at Whitson's hands, Josiah couldn't guess. "Come ahead to the cabin. My wife will tend to you."

≈

Sally stirred the pot of beans another time, hoping Pa would come in for a bite of lunch soon. When would Nathaniel return, and would Josiah and Solomon come with him? *Stop thinking about Josiah.* Nellie would tell a tall tale for sure if she could read Sally's thoughts.

"I'll keep an eye on the beans," Ma told Sally. "Go remind your pa that lunch is waiting. He overdoes it when the weather is fine like it is today."

Sally smiled, checked her mobcap—why, she couldn't say, unless she hoped to see Josiah—and opened the door. Brilliant sunshine blinded her for a moment. In the field, she saw the figures of five men outlined in black against the sun. One of them was injured.

Josiah. Sally started running.

two

Only a moment passed before Sally realized her error, but she lived a thousand lifetimes in that one second. Nathaniel and the others had returned with a stranger. She tucked a few stray hairs under her mobcap and went back inside.

"That was quickly done. Is your father on the way in?"

"He is. With an injured man."

"Nathaniel?" Ma's face blanched, and she put her hand over her dress where a new life grew within her. "An accident?"

Sally regretted causing her mother worry. "Not Nathaniel. A stranger. Perhaps someone was injured at the celebration today."

That suggestion did little to relieve Ma's worry. She sank into a chair. "A battle, do you think?" Even though a Patriot, Ma was like all mothers everywhere, Sally supposed. No one liked to see their sons go to war with the knowledge they might never return.

Ma's weakness alarmed Sally. "The others appear unharmed." Ma should eat soon, lest she faint, and not wait on the men. Unable to keep food down with the new babe on the way, she didn't eat much in the morning these days. And Pa had delayed longer than usual to come in for lunch. Sally dished up a bowl of beans and handed it to her. "Go ahead."

Ma started to protest before she accepted the wisdom of Sally's suggestion. One bite of corn bread and beans followed the next as she polished her bowl.

15

When they saw Ma eating, Nellie and Stephen rushed to the table. "You'll have to wait," Sally said. "We've got company coming."

"Who?" Nellie rushed to the door before Sally could answer.

"Nathaniel has returned with a stranger. And the Tuttles will be joining us, as well." Sally could sense heat creeping into her cheeks. Why did she feel embarrassed? It was the neighborly thing to do.

Before Nellie replied, the door opened, and Nathaniel came through, supporting a man who appeared almost unconscious. Sally strained to think of a time she had seen someone so badly beaten; even the last time Stephen had tackled Nathaniel in an all-out tussle, neither had been so bruised. Perhaps Ma's assessment of a battle had hit the mark. Blood and mud smeared on the others' breeches and shirts. Behind her, she heard her mother's gasp.

"Don't worry, my dear." Mr. Reid came up behind the younger men and placed a gentle hand on her arm. "No one is hurt except this unfortunate soul. Nathaniel offered our care for him while he recovers."

"Of course." Color returned to Ma's face, and she stood. "Sally, I'll take over serving the meal while you prepare a bed for our guest."

"His name is Schyler Van Dyke, from New York," Josiah added. "We can make more formal introductions when he regains consciousness."

A passing regret at losing the opportunity to share a word with the young Mr. Tuttle bothered Sally, but she let it go. The need for a soft bed, and not hard ground, for Mr. Van Dyke's broken body took precedence over all else.

"I'll help." Nellie skipped up the ladder, with Sally following. When they reached the top, she whispered in Sally's ear. "That way, you can finish in time to sit with Josiah."

Sally peeked over the edge, but no one was paying attention. Nellie's whisper carried across a room, loud enough for anyone to hear if they wanted to.

In answer, Sally removed the bedding from the straw tick they slept on at night. They could sleep on loose straw until Van Dyke was better. After rolling the mattress into a large ball, Sally considered how to get it to the floor below. She couldn't throw it, not with four tall men crowding around the table. For covering. . .at least the weather had grown warm. They wouldn't miss the extra blanket. She wrapped a blanket over her arm and started down the ladder. "Hand the tick down to me when I reach the floor," she told Nellie.

The problem with that plan soon became apparent. Nellie could only dangle over the edge so far without risking a fall. Sally climbed one rung, then two, and stretched. If she could at least hold the bottom. . .

"Let me." Josiah's deep voice interrupted her thoughts. Taller than her by a good ten inches, he stood flat-footed and caught the tick as Nellie dropped it. "Where do you want me to place it?" His voice sounded odd, muffled behind the burden he carried.

The only possible spot was next to her parents' bed. As long as they had company, the space was crowded, but they still could manage. "Over there." She pointed.

Without further ado, Josiah carried the bundle to the corner and spread the tick on the floor. Sally knelt beside him and tucked a linen sheet over the corners and plumped up a feather pillow to create as soft a bed as possible. In spite of his injuries, the man appeared good-sized and well built. She hoped the hay would cushion his weight. What had caused the man's injuries?

❧

"What happened?" Sally asked.

Josiah wondered how often he would retell the morning's events. "Some of the boys didn't like Mr. Van Dyke's line of work."

"Plotting land for people from New York?"

He nodded. If only explaining it to Father would come as easily. Father would demand further information until he had wrung every last detail from his sons—including the fact they had gathered to celebrate the conquest of Fort Ticonderoga. Only last week he had commented that Josiah was under his authority as long as he lived under his roof. He wouldn't countenance support of the rebellion in any son of his.

But for now, Josiah would enjoy these few stolen moment with Sally. She tucked a strand of hair, the color of wheat at harvesttime, under her mobcap. Did she realize how often she did that? Today, as always, she gave of herself to others first, forgoing lunch to serve her guests. He should send her back to his place at the table, but selfishly, he wanted her to stay.

All too soon, she finished smoothing out the bed. "It's ready." She rose, and he stepped closer. "Bring him over."

Nathaniel jumped up from the table. Van Dyke sat slumped against the wall where they had left him. Together, Josiah and Nathaniel lifted him to his feet. The surveyor awakened long enough to murmur "What. . ." But his head fell back against the ticking as soon as they laid him down.

Nathaniel reached in his waistcoat pocket for a small packet. "I brought back some willow bark."

"Good." Sally nodded in approval. "That will be useful if he develops a fever."

"Josiah?" Solomon stood and wiped the sleeve of his shirt across his mouth. "We'd best be getting home."

Josiah grimaced. The time of reckoning had come.

"Wait a moment." Mr. Reid left the table and grabbed his tricorne. "I'll go with you to discuss the morning's happenings with your father. We can't allow the Maple Notch contingent of Green Mountain Boys to go unchecked."

"We'd welcome your company." The presence of a third party might delay the explosion that was sure to come. As divided as their opinions about the revolution were, the community united on the need for the local militia. Since Maple Notch had been settled after the close of the Treaty of 1763, the militia had protected them against Indian attacks and a renewal of the hostilities with the French. Only differences of opinion over the identity of the enemy separated the community now.

The path home sped as quickly as the trek from Whitson's farm had lagged. The short walk didn't allow Josiah enough time to fashion an explanation that might calm their father's anger. His steps slowed as they entered the clearing near the cabin.

"Does your father know where you were today?" Mr. Reid must have sensed Josiah's hesitation; he knew their father's stance on the revolution.

The brothers exchanged an uneasy glance. "He knows we were with the militia." Josiah didn't add any more.

"But not what you were doing, eh?" Mr. Reid shook his head. "I'm sure he knows the significance of this date."

Had he pretended ignorance for the sake of peace? Josiah hadn't considered that possibility.

"Tory or Patriot, it doesn't matter in this case." When Reid spoke, Josiah didn't know if he was reassuring himself or the younger men. "No responsible man will stomach the kind of show young Whitson put on today."

The field stood empty, heaping mounds of planted seed in straight rows crossing the ground between stumps. Father was cleaning his hoe when the three of them came near the barn.

"Decided to come home after all, did you?" In spite of the harsh words, Father's expression was calm.

Some of the uneasiness drained from Josiah. Their late arrival hadn't raised Father's ire. He had expected them home before nooning.

"Reid, what brings you here?" Father greeted their neighbor.

"There was an incident at the gathering this morning." Reid nodded at Josiah to pick up the tale.

Once again, Josiah repeated the story, hoping it was for the last time. He emphasized the discovery of the surveyor and left out the presence of corn whiskey that had fueled the beatings.

"Hmph." Father looked as though he wished he could lash at something. "These were militia boys, you say?"

Josiah hesitated. He didn't want everyone to get in trouble. "Brad Whitson was the ringleader."

"That one's always been trouble. Who else?"

Josiah didn't want to name names. Some of the boys present followed Whitson like proverbial sheep. Beside him, Solomon shuffled his feet.

"You didn't take part in it, did you?" Father's voice held a knife's edge.

"Of course not!" What did Father think of him, to ask such a question?

"From what I understand, Josiah and Solomon stepped in to stop the carnage. With my boy's help." Reid, for one, spoke of his son with pride.

"Come in and we'll figure out what to do over a cup of tea."

Mother met them in the yard, drawing cool water from the depths of their well. After their day's exertions, even the elixir of life couldn't have tasted any better.

Bothersome black flies buzzed around Josiah's head, heedless of his attempts to brush them off. He splashed cold water over his face and joined the others in the cabin. He and Solomon remained standing while his parents and Mr. Reid took seats on the rough-hewn bench.

"Do you think we should tell the commander? Make it a matter of military discipline?" Reid suggested.

That's wise. Invite Father's opinion first. Josiah watched how the two old friends would iron out this situation.

"No need for that. We can handle this locally." Father's face reddened.

"Now, Mr. Tuttle." Mother poured out tea. "You remember what the doctor said after you had that apoplectic fit last year. Avoid upset, or it could happen again."

Father waved that aside. "Not even Whitson Senior would approve of beating up an unarmed man. We'll settle it at the next drill. Decide what punishment is appropriate." Father spoke with authority. Whatever the topic, he always had a strong opinion and wasn't afraid to voice it.

Even if no one else agreed with him.

❧

The next drill didn't take place for several weeks. Sally waited until Nathaniel and Pa had left before she took out the extra dried apple pies and rollie-polies she had made for today's picnic. Nellie had giggled so much all morning that Sally felt sure Nathaniel would guess their surprise. Once or twice, she had been tempted to giggle herself, but she restrained herself. A young woman of seventeen now, she practiced an adult demeanor—even when planning a party.

Van Dyke had planted the idea in the ladies' heads. The first day he felt well enough to sit at the table, Ma had baked pie. He ate every bite and even accepted the one leftover slice. "That was truly stupendous. My mother could make me do almost anything for a piece of her dried apple pie."

A light beamed from Ma's eyes, indicating his offhand comment had brought a plan to mind. Later Sally asked, "What're you thinking?"

"Why, how everybody enjoys a party. When there's good food, fellowship, and games, people feel too good to put up a fuss. I think it's time Maple Notch had a party."

Sally could guess the direction of Ma's thinking. "And the perfect time might be next Monday, when the militia gets together to drill?"

"And when the circuit preacher will be here for Rogation Day. It's the perfect time. I'll spread word among the town's womenfolk."

Rogation Day. Of course. Although usually planned for a Sunday, Maple Notch celebrated the day when the crops were blessed whenever their preacher was available. So the plan was born. Ma had fretted when Pa told her they intended to confront the miscreants at the next drill. The Whitsons, both father and son, were as likely to pull a knife or a musket when threatened as to listen to reason. Now, God willing, she might thwart the possibility before it arose.

All their preparations completed, the Reids made ready to depart. Sally paused long enough to speak with their guest. "Are you certain you don't mind staying alone?" Van Dyke had recovered enough to sit for short periods of time, but everyone agreed he'd best stay close to the farm. "We'll set aside a chunk of the pie just for you."

"I'm fine, Miss Reid. I'm sorry to have been the cause of such discord in your town."

"No one is blaming you for men's wicked ways, Mr. Van Dyke. I am sure you will be glad to leave us behind as soon as you are able." Sally tied her hair back with a pink ribbon before putting on her mobcap. *Vanity,* she thought. *Using Ma's best ribbon to show off your hair, because once Josiah mentioned how pretty you looked in pink.*

"Are we ready?" Ma had regained some of her vigor over the last few weeks, now that the difficult days of morning sickness had passed. According to her, these were the best months of pregnancy, before the ever-increasing weight of the baby sapped her of strength. She insisted she felt well enough to go to the picnic with them.

When Nellie appeared, a bit of flour smudged the elbow of her dress, but otherwise she was clean. Sally's little sister preferred outside play to working in the kitchen, and she was almost harder to keep clean than the menfolk.

The men drilled at the usual spot, on the town common. With Tory and Patriot alike coming together to address the problem of the surveyor, the area would be crowded. Ma tucked a couple of blankets under her arm, and Sally carried the heavy basket. They entrusted a small jar of buttermilk to Nellie.

A pale sun took the chill off the air and dried the dew from the grass under their feet. The grass had grown tall enough to brush the hems of their skirts. Sally thought about kicking off her shoes and running stocking-footed in the grass, but that would rip her newly mended hose and stain them beyond redemption.

Once they reached the river, she studied the water's flow. Not as high as it had been during spring runoffs. She decided to remove her shoes and hose long enough to cross. First Nellie skipped across, as surefooted as a deer on the mountains. Ma followed, placing her feet with care on each stone and handing the blanket ahead to Nellie. Last of all, Sally bent over at the riverbank, tugging at her shoes and hose.

"Sally." Ma's tone carried reprimand enough.

"No one's here to see." She placed her footwear on top of the basket, lifted her skirts with one hand, and waded in. Cool, delicious water caressed her skin, easing away dirt and soreness, even if she stubbed her toes on a rock or two. She squelched mud between her toes and then circled her ankles about to clean them of the day's dust.

Ma shook her head. "You're setting a bad example for Nellie. And what if someone came by while you had lifted your skirts? Anyone could have seen your ankles."

Sally looked around. "Where?" Seeing no one about, she pulled up her hose and laced her shoes. "There. All set to go."

"I'd like to do that on the trip back," Nellie whispered when Ma fell behind.

"Don't you dare. She'd tan me for sure." Sally smiled to

let Nellie know she wasn't serious. Her sister hid her smile. Nellie could be a lot of fun.

They had forded the river close to town, and soon they approached the common. A ring of men surrounded Brad Whitson, his father, and a handful of other rough-and-ready farmers. The stern faces of watching men told Sally they hadn't arrived a moment too soon.

Josiah and Solomon stood with their backs to the women, two young saplings growing into tall trees. Mr. Tuttle continued to tower over them, although Josiah was fast coming up to the same size.

Approaching from the other direction, Sally spotted Martha Whitson, Brad's likeable sister, and her mother. They didn't want an argument any more than the Reids did. Other women of the town gathered. Josiah's head turned, as if the unexpected arrival of company distracted him. He said something in his father's ear that Sally couldn't hear.

"What's this?" Pa called out loud enough to be heard. Everyone in the circle looked in one direction, then another at the women carrying blankets and baskets.

"It's a surprise picnic, Mr. Reid." Ma moved more quickly than Sally expected for a woman in her condition. "To celebrate Rogation Day." Her voice held the same honey-coated knife's edge that kept her children in line most of the time.

A smile creased Josiah's face. "Gentlemen, I say, let's welcome the ladies."

three

Josiah walked straight in Sally's direction, and she sucked in her breath. Solomon looked at their father, shrugged, and trotted over to stand beside Martha Whitson. Soon every man found a lady of his choosing, a welcome development of the picnic.

"Don't think we're through." Sally overheard Mr. Tuttle growl at the Whitsons. Their animosity ran deep, stemming from issues existing long before the surveyor entered the picture. They'd fought over politics for years, since well before Independence.

But on this beautiful, sunshiny day, the women of Maple Notch had accomplished what they'd intended. Rogation Day, with the blessing of the crops and later the beating of the borders, would unite them in a celebration of the unique heritage that brought Maple Notch into being.

Josiah reached her side and took a blanket from her, spreading it across the grass. She sat down and kept her gaze on the ground. Was he seeking her out? Or perhaps he had joined the family group closest to him on the green. That was it, nothing more. She allowed herself a quick peek as she handed him a slice of cheese.

His gaze settled on her face, and she felt a blush creep above the collar of her dress. "Do I have a piece of cheese stuck to my teeth?"

He grinned at her. "No. Your teeth are fine. I'm sorry if I was rude."

She reached for a strand of hair that had strayed from the bow and tucked it behind her ear.

Ma stretched out a second blanket next to theirs, close enough to keep an eye on them but far enough away to give them some privacy. Sally saw Nellie whisper something in their mother's ear before giggling. Someone might as well post a sign above their heads stating "courting couple."

At least Josiah didn't notice, or if he did, he didn't seem to mind. Maybe he had wanted that to happen. The thought made the cheese turn dry in Sally's throat.

"How is Van Dyke?" Josiah managed a normal voice. He didn't seem aware of all the eyes following them.

"He's f–fine." She stammered, something she never did. "In fact, Pa thinks he'll be well enough to travel within a fortnight."

"You must be an accomplished herbalist, if he has already recovered from that beating." Josiah picked a dandelion from the grass and held it to his nose. "If you can make a tasty dish from dandelion greens, you must know other of nature's hidden treasures " He dug into the crock that held the referenced dish. " 'Tis one of springtime's pleasures."

"Every woman knows how to cook greens. Ma knows a lot more about medicinal plants than I do." Sally shied away from the praise. "And of course we've been praying for him, for his healing. . .and safety."

"It's best if Van Dyke leaves as soon as he's able." Josiah nodded toward Whitson. "He's embarrassed about what happened, and would as soon take it out on someone."

That's why we came today. To prevent an incident. But Sally didn't voice their concerns. No need to worry Josiah further. Men did what they felt they had to do, and many times women coped with the aftermath. Instead, she said, "And he may have family worried about him. We haven't been able to send word. Not with the British threatening to cut off Lake Champlain."

"Seems like New York would have enough to keep them busy with General Burgoyne breathing down their necks." Josiah dug into the greens again. "Why they'd bother sending out a surveyor to Vermont at a time like this. . .it doesn't make sense."

"Do you think he'll succeed?" Sally shivered. With Canada across the border and the approach of the British from Lake Champlain, Maple Notch was vulnerable to capture.

"I'm not the best person to ask. People don't tell me much." Josiah's brown eyes dulled to a dark gray as he looked at the gathered townsfolk. "Things look civilized at the moment, but as soon as the topic of the fight against the British comes up. . .might as well build a wall between us."

"How do you cope with your father?" Sally couldn't imagine the difficulties Josiah faced with their differences.

Josiah let out a low, bitter laugh. "We don't talk much, that's how—beyond discussing what crops to plant and which fields he wants worked. The Patriots won't talk to me because they're afraid I'll tell my father, and he won't talk to me for fear I'll tell the Patriots."

The loneliness evident on Josiah's face cut Sally to the quick. Perhaps she and Ma should visit Mrs. Tuttle. At least Josiah had Solomon, and so far, Mr. Tuttle allowed them to drill with the militia. They got to see other people. But their mother might feel cut off. "Do your parents agree? About the British?"

Her ma and pa were of one mind about the Revolution.

Ma didn't like fighting, but she believed in the Patriots' cause. Unless Britain listened to reason, armed conflict seemed the only option.

"I don't know. The one time I asked her, she said she planned to submit to his authority, in accordance with the Word of God."

Spoken like a true Tory.

"Enough about the war. We can find more pleasant topics to discuss." Josiah bit into the crust of the dried apple pie.

They sat in silence. Sally cast her mind about, looking for a topic, *any* topic, that had nothing to do with the war. Her mind remained as blank as a child's slate on the first day of school. *Oh, yes.* "There's an owl building a nest in the rafters of our barn." An owl would be as good as a cat in hunting down any mice that might threaten their grain.

"That's good. We used to have an owl nearby, but he's taken off." Josiah grinned. "Maybe the same one that's taken up residence in your barn."

Silence stretched between them again until Josiah spoke. "Planting is going well this year. The beans and corn are sprouting fast."

"That's what Pa says. He hopes we get a bumper crop."

They chatted about the weather, the proper amount of seed to use, the prospects of the growing season. Safe topics. Boring topics. Topics of interest to farmers, more immediate concerns than battles and independence.

The sun moved high overhead in the sky and would soon begin its journey westward. The circuit preacher, accompanied by Elder Cabot, called them together for Rogation festivities. Around them, people repacked baskets with whatever remained, folded blankets, and prepared to leave. After an afternoon in Josiah's presence, even if they had spoken of everyday, mundane things, Sally didn't want to return to the farm. But she mustn't dawdle any longer.

So far they had avoided the one topic closest to her heart. With her face averted so that Josiah wouldn't see her telltale blush and think her overly bold, she asked, "Do you think your father will let you go, if the Green Mountain Boys are called upon to fight in this war for independence?"

"I. . .don't know. No, he won't agree. But I haven't decided how I will respond."

Sally sneaked a look at him, but like her, he had averted his face. Only the tension in his neck muscles, the way he jutted his chin, betrayed the turmoil he must be feeling. Since Fort Ticonderoga fell without a fight, the Vermont militia hadn't done much to prove themselves. Sally had little doubt that they would be drawn into battle sooner or later.

"I'm praying for you. For all the families that have that choice to make. For our town."

"As are we all." Josiah stood and brushed down his breeches, scattering crumbs for gathering grouse. They joined the other townsfolk following the preacher as he walked around the village, asking God for a bountiful harvest. Then everyone headed home.

After the two families crossed the river, the rogation antics began. The four young men took turns bumping each other into the boundary stone and later the fence that separated the two farms. By now, all of them could probably walk the boundary between their property blindfolded.

The family groups walked away, giving Sally a moment of privacy with Josiah. "Thank you for a delicious meal," he said. "It was well thought." They stopped under the overhanging branches of a willow tree, where she turned her face up to his.

"Ma did most of the cooking."

"I'll speak with Father about Solomon and me accompanying Mr. Van Dyke back to New York. Neither my brother nor I want him encountering another party intent on harm."

Sally's heart fluttered at the thought. What dangers might await Josiah on the road? She kept her worries to herself. "I'll let Pa know. We'll send a message when our guest is able to travel."

❧

Josiah brushed at the mosquitoes that buzzed around any exposed patches of skin, far worse here than in Maple Notch. Transporting Van Dyke to his home via Lake Champlain had seemed like a good plan when Solomon had suggested it. Once on the water, Josiah wasn't so sure. Every insect in two states decided to feast on them en route. He also remembered rumors of General Burgoyne's progress in his plans to attack New York via the lake. So far, they'd had a peaceful journey and avoided any larger boats.

Today they expected to pass under the nose of Fort Ticonderoga and determine a portage to Lake George, from where Van Dyke promised the travel to his home was but a long day's hike through the woods. Once they reached the fort, Josiah felt he could relax. "There it is," Van Dyke called from the back of the canoe. "The path to the fort lies in that direction."

The sun glinted off the granite walls of the fort, making it hard for Josiah to see any details. He remembered tales from those who participated in the '75 campaign. Those brave souls had gone after a British fort before independence had been declared. Foolish, his father had said.

The fort, shaped like a misshapen star, derived its name from an Indian word meaning "where two waterways meet"—lakes Champlain and George. No wonder both sides valued the strategic location.

As one, Solomon and Josiah paddled toward the shore the fort guarded. As they approached, the reflected image of the buildings shimmered in the water. Red roofs peaked above high walls, red as blood, although thankfully none had been shed in the taking of the fort. It looked strong, stalwart—a symbol of America's strength and confidence. "Thou art our fortress."

"Do you think they'll take us in for the night?" Josiah asked Van Dyke, cocking his head toward the fort.

"They allowed me to stay on my way north." Van Dyke smiled at the memory before grimacing. "They won't be pleased with the reception I received. The lands along the border are essential to protection from invasion by the British from Canada."

"We can defend our own!" Solomon protested.

"The Continental Congress—and the state of New York— believes that the more of an American presence we establish along the northern frontiers, the more secure we are."

Josiah smarted inside. Did Van Dyke know Father supported the crown? That if the British invaded, he would be the first to join their ranks? More importantly, if that happened, what would Josiah do? How could he honor his father when he believed with all his heart that Father was wrong? Even the thought of his sons spending the night at an American fort would upset him.

Van Dyke guided them through milfoil and water chestnuts toward the bank, where trees grew so dense Josiah didn't see how even a fox could squeeze through. The canoe glided underneath the cool canopy, the lake only a slender line of blue through branches blurred by foliage. "There it is. The path I told you about." The only evidence was a few bent twigs.

"How can we carry the canoe?" Solomon looked at the growth in front of them. Even if they could maneuver the load through the forest, they would mark a path so wide that even a blind man could make his way to the fort.

The three men looked about them. "If we continue around the bend, will we find a better place to make the portage?" Josiah inquired of Van Dyke, since he had made the trip earlier.

"A little ways farther down the lake."

"Then we'll leave it here and come back for it tomorrow." Josiah decided. The three of them made quick work of hiding the canoe under branches and leaves. Where the birch bark shone through, it blended with the surrounding trees.

To give the man credit, Van Dyke hadn't slowed them down on their trip. He appeared to have made a complete recovery from the beating he had received. More strength resided in his arm muscles than Josiah had guessed upon first meeting him at Whitson's farm. Throughout the journey, the surveyor had proved helpful on several occasions. In fact, if Van Dyke hadn't come to Vermont on such a hated mission, Josiah would have warmed up to him sooner. But hadn't General Washington been a surveyor once upon a time? Josiah shouldn't hold Van Dyke's profession against him.

The men picked up their few belongings, a musket slung over each man's shoulders, and began the climb. They didn't speak, at first from caution, then because the path steepened. Even as work-toughened as Josiah was, he needed breath for each step. In the quiet stillness of the forest, he could scarce believe a fort filled with battle-ready soldiers lay ahead. The peace could fool him into thinking everything was right with God's world. A warbler sang out, and its mate returned the call. Chickadees darted in and out of the trees, as well as a dozen others he couldn't name. Every now and then, deer tracks crossed their own. The fort should be well supplied, provided they could gain access to these woods.

About midway up the incline, Josiah caught sight of a patch of red. Only the male cardinal sported that bright color. *God loves colors.* He could imagine Sally's voice. *See how He splashes it around creation.*

The same red flashed again, and this time he could see this was no bird. He stiffened. Behind him, Solomon stopped. He whistled, a low bobolink's call, the agreed upon signal to get Van Dyke's attention. The man froze in his tracks before turning around with a questioning glance.

Solomon was already heading in the direction of the Redcoat. He could move almost as quietly as an Indian through the forest, certainly better than the field-trained soldier who now thrashed his way through the underbrush like a bull on a rampage.

Josiah wanted to call his brother back. Rash, impulsive, Solomon might be, but he should know better than to approach the man. Where there was one soldier, there might be more. But Josiah didn't dare call out, not when he might reveal their presence to the soldier. Perhaps he was a scout, sent ahead. General Burgoyne's drive through New York surfaced in his mind again.

Josiah inched forward. The man neared the trail, which, as faint as it was, might still attract his attention. He must be stopped.

Solomon was almost close enough to touch the soldier when a crow dropped from the sky, screeching, talons missing his face by inches. He cried out but once, but the soldier turned at the sound, bayonet poised for battle. Before Solomon could position his musket in his hands, the Redcoat brought him to the ground with his weapon.

All thoughts of caution fled Josiah's mind. With a single, fluid motion, he raised his musket and plunged through the few yards of forest remaining. He paused in midstep to aim and fired. The ball hit the Redcoat, and he collapsed.

Josiah ran past his crumpled body to reach Solomon's side. Already, his brother was gasping for breath.

"Must warn. . .the fort."

"You need a doctor."

"Leave me here." Solomon's eyelashes fluttered at him, his dark eyes clouding as he forced words through his throat. "It's too late for me."

Van Dyke joined them. "No one else has come. It appears no one heard the shot."

In his worry, Josiah had forgotten about the possibility of other soldiers in the vicinity.

"Go. Before. They. Come." Solomon forced each word through his throat with effort.

"I won't leave you." Josiah gripped Solomon's hand with his own.

"I'll go. But first, let's move farther into the trees. Away from. . ." Van Dyke gestured at the carnage around them. Josiah thought of the birds that would soon circle overhead and the evidence of the battle. But the bayonet had skewered Solomon's body to the ground. Removing it would hasten his death.

"No, you go on ahead. We'll—" Josiah's voice broke. "We'll catch up as soon as we can."

"I'll hide the Redcoat, then. When you're ready, the trail is right over there." Van Dyke placed a hand on Josiah's shoulder and then trotted away.

Solomon's every breath was a titanic struggle, but the sound pleased Josiah more than the sweetest bird's song he had ever heard. Each gasp meant his brother still lived. He knelt by Solomon's side and searched for words. He should pray, but what for? That time would go backwards? That he could have taken the bayonet instead of Solomon? That they had never decided to go to the fort? That God would somehow, someway intervene and prevent the obvious from happening?

"Tell Father. . ."

"No last words." *I refuse to listen.*

"I'm sorry." In the depths of Solomon's eyes, he looked older than the elders of Maple Notch and held all the mysteries of life in his hand. "Say. . .a psalm," Solomon begged.

The words of Psalm 23 sprang to Josiah's mouth: "The Lord is my shepherd; I shall not want. He maketh me to lie down in green pastures. . . ." David could have been speaking of the glade where they waited, green with the new growth of spring. Josiah stumbled, willing himself not to cry.

A smile replaced the pain on Solomon's face, and his grasp on Josiah's hand relaxed. As Josiah recited the final words of the psalm—"And I will dwell in the house of the Lord for ever"—Solomon slipped away into that eternal rest.

four

"The British are approaching Fort Ticonderoga." Nathaniel preceded his father into their cabin with the news.

Sally stopped chopping the carrot in front of her. "They're *here*—in Vermont?"

"Near here."

Sally's eyes drifted to Ma, who looked at Pa with a resigned expression. "When will you be leaving?"

"Our militia will meet at sundown. We'll leave by sunrise, if not before. We'll travel light." He looked at Nathaniel, who straightened his shoulders and looked very grown-up, in spite of his scant sixteen years. "Your Ma would like you to stay home."

Sally held her breath. Surely Nathaniel wouldn't go; he was hardly more than a child. . .a year younger than herself. The same age as Solomon Tuttle, who had left home on an important mission.

Ma placed a hand on her abdomen, where the coming child was becoming obvious, and sat down without speaking.

"I practice with the militia."

When had Nathaniel's voice deepened so that he sounded so much like Pa that it hurt?

"What good is drilling if I don't fight?" Nathaniel's face set in determined lines.

A moan escaped Ma's lips.

Pa put his hand on Nathaniel's shoulder. "It is your decision, son. All I ask is that you talk it over with God before you make up your mind." He patted him awkwardly on the back. "I will finish the chores for the day while you think about what to do."

Nathaniel looked at Ma, then at Sally. "I'll do as he says. I'll go down by the creek and pray. But I already know the answer." His shoulders filled the doorway as he walked outside.

Sally put her arms around Ma. "Whatever shall we do, Ma?"

She spread her fingers far apart as if to measure the distance between them. "Why, we'll trust God and do our patriotic duty. I knew this day was coming as soon as we heard about Lexington and Concord."

Sally wanted to storm outside and scream. Tears formed in her eyes.

"None of that." Ma spoke in gentle tones. "I wish I hadn't been so weak just now. We need to be strong for the men. For the children."

Sally wondered if Nellie would worry. Young Stephen would wish he were old enough to go with them. She was grateful they were fishing by the river today and had a few more hours of peace until they heard the news. Would they see Nathaniel? Would he tell them what had happened?

True to her word, Ma roused herself from the table and gathered a few simple foodstuffs the men could carry easily. What did they consider basic supplies? Would they want a covering if the nights grew cold? Flint for fire, a skein for water, a pan to cook in, perhaps? A change of clothes? Definitely a powder horn and bullet mold. Sally could think of a hundred things they could use and only a handful of things that were truly necessary. She showed Ma what she had assembled.

"You've shown good sense." Ma examined the supplies Sally had laid out while she had whipped together a batch of corn pone. "I won't let them leave without eating something. Who knows when they'll have their next hot meal?" She rubbed her nose but stopped short of a sniffle.

Pa came in early from the fields, followed by Nellie and Stephen. Nellie looked sad enough to cry, Stephen so excited that he would burst if he couldn't talk. Pa must have warned them to keep quiet, because they went to a corner in the room and talked between themselves.

Nathaniel followed not half a minute later. "I'm going." He didn't expound.

Pa's eyes sought out his wife. "Mary." The look that passed between Sally's parents was the same one she longed to see from her husband's face some day. Understanding, love, support—regret. Pa led Ma by the hand to their bed and hung a blanket from a rope for privacy. The murmur of their voices told Sally her parents were exchanging words of farewell, of love and longing—intimacies they didn't care to exchange in front of the children. Sally chased Stephen and Nellie outside.

The pone had finished baking by the time Ma and Pa pulled the blanket down and called the family to the table. Stephen and Nellie were bickering, but Ma didn't seem to have the heart to interrupt. Pa spoke in a voice low enough for only Sally to hear.

"Sally. I'm depending on you to keep things going around here. Stephen may need help with the fields. I'm sure you'll know what to do." He sighed.

Sally nodded while her mind raced. Danger could assail them without Pa or Nathaniel to protect them. She remembered Ma's words. *Be strong.* "God will be with us." She said it with more confidence than she felt. The words of Holy Scripture would become more than words spoken by rote before this was over, she feared.

"And Sally?" Pa made her look at him.

"Yes, Pa?" She blinked to keep tears from falling.

"Josiah Tuttle's a good man. When he returns, ask him for help if you need it." Pa kissed the top of her head, and Sally felt she had received his blessing.

All too soon, Pa and Nathaniel took their leave. Sally looked at her brother, at his fierce expression, and flung her arms around him. He stiffened, then relented and returned the embrace. The touch expressed everything Sally dared not put into words. She joined Ma and the younger children at the door, watching as Pa and Nathaniel crossed the yard, the fields. . .until they were little more than a speck against the encroaching forest. Nellie hiccupped a sob and ran inside.

Sally's thoughts strayed to Josiah and Solomon, thankful they were absent from Maple Notch, and not facing the terrible dilemma of their father's opposition.

❧

Josiah could have stayed by Solomon's side all night. He could have run screaming into the forest, hoping to awake and discover it was all a nightmare. But he didn't have the luxury for the first choice or the imagination for the second.

Not relishing the task, Josiah pulled the bayonet from Solomon's still body. In life, his brother had been nigh on to Josiah's own height, and only a few pounds lighter. The additional weight would double the path's difficulty, but Josiah would not, could not leave his brother behind. What had Van Dyke done with the Redcoat? He thought he caught sight of a patch of red beneath an uprooted tree, underneath pines and dead leaves. No one would notice it if he wasn't searching for it.

The color in the sky, drained by the trees, had grown even darker while Josiah finished his tasks. He hurried to reach the fort before night fell, even if it was only days past midsummer's eve. More and more branches hit his legs and arms and face when he could no longer make out the path. In the distance, he saw flames burning atop Mount Independence, suggestive of the battle the single soldier represented.

The conflagration provided light enough for Josiah to make out the gate to the fort straight ahead. The sight gave strength to his tired legs, and he ran as though a fiery wind blew him to safety. Panting, he arrived at the door. An eye appeared in a peephole. "Halt! Who goes there!"

"A Patriot," Josiah managed to stammer. "Of Maple Notch."

The eye disappeared, and the door swung open to reveal a young soldier in a makeshift uniform, much the same age as himself. "Van Dyke said to expect you. That you escorted him here from the north." Then he took note of the burden Josiah carried. "What happened?"

"My brother." Josiah's voice caught in his throat. "We came upon a Redcoat on the path. Solomon charged him and caught his bayonet." Josiah told the few, sad facts, as he scanned the inside of the compound. In light of the British threat, he'd expected the place to teem with soldiers. Even with his limited knowledge of battle strategy, the fort seemed poorly garrisoned. Perhaps twice their number could defend the fort.

"Major General St. Clair will want to speak with you."

"My brother—" Josiah recognized the need to inform St.

Clair. He must be in command, although he wondered what had happened to Gates. But the burial of his brother took priority.

The sentry's face softened. "I will arrange for him to be placed in the infirmary. We cannot leave the fort to bury him until dawn, if then." He paused. "If the commander permits, you may go there after you speak with him and make whatever preparations you wish."

Since Josiah was at the soldier's mercy, he agreed and headed in the direction of the major general's headquarters. A soldier blocked his entry until Van Dyke called out a greeting.

"Here's our man." Van Dyke sounded relieved.

Josiah wondered what sort of grilling the commander had subjected him to and what he himself now faced.

"Tuttle, is it? One of Ethan Allen's Green Mountain Boys?"

"Yes, sir."

St. Clair studied him. "Are the militia on the move? From Maple Notch, or elsewhere?"

"Not when we left, sir."

The man paced the small room. Maps studded the walls, splashed with red flags Josiah guessed represented the British. St. Clair's pacing had a frantic quality to it, as if he could find the path to victory in battle if he moved fast enough. The major general collected himself and stopped long enough to face Josiah directly. "I understand your brother was mortally wounded tonight by a British soldier. And that you responded bravely. I thank you for your service."

The look St. Clair directed at him focused all the rage and anguish roiling inside of Josiah. Without thought, he blurted,

"I wish to stay here and fight, sir."

A thin smile played around the commander's lips. "Very well, Tuttle. I will consider your offer. We will have need of all the good men we can muster in the next few days, and Allen's militia has earned a good reputation."

Dismissed, Josiah checked on Solomon's remains. He wished he had a change of clothes to put on his body. After closing his brother's eyes and crossing his arms across his chest, Josiah did what he could to prepare him for burial. A lump formed in his throat. He had no way to alert the family to his death, to let news of the impending ceremony spread throughout the community so they could gather for a funeral dinner. What would he say to Father to explain what had happened? Guilt rained down on him like a thunderstorm in its intensity. He could think of only one person who might understand, who would at least listen without censure. *Sally.*

Josiah tarried by Solomon's side long enough to say a prayer for him, for himself, for all those who faced battle on the morrow. Then he approached the sentry who stood guard at the door.

"Do you have any scrip and quill that I can use?"

The man looked as though he would make a humorous remark but refrained when he glanced at the dead body. "I'm sure I can find something. Come, let me show you where you will spend the night.

A few men sat across the floor of the room where the guard conducted him. Soft snores suggested a few slumbered, while others read or wrote by candlelight. Josiah found a space near a wall sconce and propped his back against the wall.

He needed rest, but he doubted any would come. Instead,

he took the time to consider what he would say to his father. As soon as he had paper and ink, he wrote the words that had formed in his mind. *Dear Sally. . . .* His heart poured out as the gloom of the night deepened.

Who knew if the letters would ever reach their intended recipients?

❧

Loud knocking rattled the door to the Reids' cabin, the sound a harbinger of anything but good news.

"Go into the loft," Sally told Nellie and Stephen. "Hurry! Now!"

The knocking repeated, and this time a loud voice called out, "Open the door in the name of the King!"

"What king?" Sally muttered to herself. Tories come to torment them while Pa was away fighting at Fort Ticonderoga. But she dared not ignore the demand.

Ma's face was whiter than the flour she was using to make bread. But she moved to the door, Sally following close behind. *Lord, protect us. Be our rock and fortress as Your Word promises.*

A group of men circled the door, every one a Tory. Ben Tuttle was not among them, which surprised Sally.

"How may I help you?"

How did Ma keep her voice so calm? Sally's voice would sound like a schoolgirl if she spoke.

Marshall Hawkins, the brawniest of the Tory men, moved forward until he stood less than a foot from Ma. "You can 'help' us by getting off this farm. We claim your land in the name of King George."

"As you know, Mr. Hawkins, we do not recognize the right of the sovereign of England to dictate what we will or will not do." Ma spoke with nary a quiver to her voice, her chin high and steady in the air.

Indignation replaced Sally's earlier fear

Hawkins moved closer still, face-to-face with Ma. "Do you think you can stand up against us?"

Sally had heard enough. She pulled Ma behind her and placed her hands on the stays of her dress. "You're as bad a bully as your son was in school, Mr. Hawkins. If you wanted to help King George, you would have joined General Burgoyne. You wouldn't be coming around here, trying to frighten a bunch of women and children." Determination to do her Pa's bidding and protect the family filled her. "We won't be pushed off our land by the likes of you."

Hawkins looked around the farmyard—at the chickens clucking in their pen, the cows angling their heads over the fence rail, the corn shooting up in the field. "This is a lot for young Stephen to keep up by himself. It would be a shame if something happened to him."

The threat was plain.

Stephen. Fear shot through Sally.

"I must insist that you leave. Now." Ma's voice remained as steady as ever. Only Sally could feel the trembling of her arm where she put it around Sally's shoulders.

"Think about what I said." Hawkins gestured to the men surrounding him. "We *will* be back."

Sally and Ma stood in the doorway while Hawkins climbed on his horse's back and the gathering galloped away, straight through the cornfield, trampling several rows of new growth. She gritted her teeth.

The younger children must have watched them leave, because they scrambled down the ladder. Nellie flung her arms around her mother, sobbing. Stephen stood tall, looking so much like Pa that Sally wanted to cry. Her little brother was a boy trying to do a man's job. At thirteen, he was too young for such responsibility.

"What shall we do?" Ma's petticoats muffled Nellie's voice.

"We'll stay and raise our crops. Right, Ma?" Stephen asked for affirmation. "We can't let those Tories stop us."

After the men left, some of the starch seeped from Ma's frame, and Sally led her to a chair. Pa expected Sally to take charge. If Pa were here, he'd fight them. But Pa wasn't here, and that was the problem. The Tories' threat endangered all the Patriot families whose men of fighting age were gone.

"Perhaps. . ." Ma swallowed the little tea left in her cup. The small drink seemed to revive her spirits, and she straightened in her chair. "I don't believe these men will hurt us. They are our neighbors, our friends." She placed a tender hand on Stephen's cheek. "If you wish to farm the fields, then of course we will stay. But it would be prudent for two of us to stay together at all times. Whether in the barn or plowing or here in the house. I know how to use a musket, if needed. Your father taught me when Indian attacks were a possibility."

Pride swelled in Sally's heart. Stephen was too young to remember the French and Indian War, and Nellie hadn't even been born then. Sally recalled several fearful nights, when they had huddled under their beds and their parents had kept guard at the windows. Ma had shown plenty of courage then, and Sally could emulate her example now. She would fight General Burgoyne himself if he showed up to threaten her family.

"I'll go milk the cows." Stephen spoke as if nothing out of the ordinary had happened.

"Remember," Ma warned.

"I'll go with him. We'll finish more quickly that way." Sally seized the opportunity.

Nellie's face crumpled as she realized she would have to stay inside.

"You can help me finish the bread," Ma said. She was so good at soothing rumpled feelings. "But we left the dough to rise too long. We may have to start over with biscuits." Nellie shrugged and covered her hands with flour.

When Sally and Stephen were heading back to the cabin after milking, a lone figure appeared on foot at the edge of the field. Ben Tuttle. *Josiah's father.* Fear rushed into Sally's heart, whether for herself or for Josiah, she couldn't say. She pointed him out to Stephen, and they hurried inside.

"Mr. Tuttle's coming," Stephen announced.

"Alone," Sally hastened to add.

"Ben Tuttle has been our neighbor for my entire married life. He means us no harm."

Ben Tuttle the neighbor might mean them no harm, but Sally wasn't so sure about Ben Tuttle the Tory. Did he come with ill tidings about Josiah—or another friendly warning?

Nellie placed the biscuits in the oven as Tuttle arrived at the door. His gentle knock let them know they had a visitor. Ma cleaned her hands on her apron, straightened her skirts, and opened the door.

"Mrs. Reid." Josiah's father doffed his hat and inclined his head. "May I come in?" His shoulders sagged, as if his sons' absence weighed on him, but his usual belligerence was absent. Sally relaxed a fraction.

"Please enter. We were about to have a bite of supper, if you would care to join us." Ma offered the same invitation she had hundreds of times before.

Tuttle smiled, a sad smile that echoed Josiah's expression but without his warmth and good humor. "I don't think that would be appropriate in the circumstances."

Fear crept back up Sally's back. "Have you news from—about Mr. Van Dyke? Has he returned to safety?"

Tuttle shook his head. "It's too soon for news. No, I came because I'm aware of Mr. Hawkins' actions this day." His chest heaved with a great sigh. "I don't agree with this declaration of independence from Britain. You know that." He twisted his hat in his hands. "I also don't agree with threats of violence against women and children, but others do. They feel any means are—acceptable—in the battle we face." He looked straight at Ma, but his gaze encompassed Sally and the children. "I would not be a good neighbor if I didn't warn you. Other Patriot families have moved into town. For your own safety, I urge the same on you."

Sally wanted to respect this man, Josiah's father, but she couldn't remain quiet. "You are little better than they are. You say you don't sanction violence, but you're after the same end. No different. You want us off our land."

"Only until this—thing—is resolved. For your safety." Tuttle pleaded.

Stephen took a step forward, but Ma restrained him. "For the sake of our long friendship, Ben, I won't speak against you. But we will not give into threats. My husband left me in charge of this land, this farm, and we will work it to the best of our ability."

Nellie crept next to Sally and glared at Mr. Tuttle.

"Thank you for your concern, Ben. But I think you'd best leave." Any hesitation Ma had shown earlier had fled.

Tuttle looked as though he would speak, then placed his hat on his head and turned to leave. He stopped long enough for one final comment before he opened the door. "Don't say I didn't warn you."

The door closed behind him with a whisper of wind.

The scent of freshly baked biscuits rose from the oven, and beans bubbled on the stove. Everyday, familiar events. Sally wondered how long they would continue.

After she served the meal, Ma led in prayer. When at last they said *amen*, she looked at each child in turn. "We need not be afraid. *God* will protect us."

But Pa isn't here. Not even Nathaniel. Sally didn't know how her mother could express such certainty.

Her own heart harbored tremendous doubts.

five

"St. Clair said *what?*" Josiah couldn't believe the command relayed to him by the guard who had greeted him upon his arrival at the fort.

"He gave the command to retreat. Both from here and from Mount Independence." The guard looked uncomfortable. "We're undermanned here. No one expected the British to drag cannon up Mount Defiance."

Perhaps, but give up the fort without a fight? Josiah couldn't imagine Ethan Allen doing such a thing. But the Green Mountain Boys weren't here, and his job under Major General St. Clair's command was to obey orders.

"I wanted to thank you again." Van Dyke, fully returned to health, found Josiah in the chaos surrounding their withdrawal from the fort. He now wore the makeshift uniform of the other soldiers. "You reminded me that there are some things worth fighting for." He glanced over his shoulder at an officer assembling his men. "Please convey my deepest sympathy to your family."

"God be with you." Josiah couldn't manage a warmer farewell. He rued the day he had ever set eyes on the New Yorker. Not that he blamed Van Dyke for the British attack on the fort, but apart from him, Solomon would never have left Maple Notch. God was sovereign, and Solomon would have given his life for his country ten times over. Nevertheless, his death seemed so pointless to Josiah. "I may

50

join you later, but first I must break the news to my father."

Van Dyke gestured at the gathering troops. "It looks like they'll have need of all who are willing. God go with you, friend." He slapped Josiah on the back before marching away with determined steps.

As instructed, Josiah departed with the soldiers. A crazy part of him wanted to stay at the fort, to descend on the incoming British with a shout and die a heroic but needless death. When he thought of his father and his own role in Solomon's death, he knew he wouldn't, even it were possible. When he thought of Sally, her sweet smile and winsome ways, he didn't want to. Not that he deserved her, or any woman, not after what he let happen to his brother. So he passed through the gates. Only instead of heading to Lake George, he turned northeast into the woods. He wouldn't attempt the lake route again. Too many unfriendly eyes might see him from the shores; now that he traveled alone, he'd stand a better chance of avoiding encounters in the woods.

The following morning after he had breakfasted on hardtack and some newly ripened strawberries, he took his bearings and headed in the direction of Maple Notch. Before long, rustling in the bushes stopped his progress. He froze and then sought cover in the crook of a tree. Last night, he could have sworn that British troops had passed by. He had slept in fits and starts, certain he would be discovered at any moment. Had reinforcements arrived?

A bobolink's distinctive call sounded—the signal for the Maple Notch militia. Someone answered. Relief flooded through Josiah. *Friends.* He pushed through the foliage in the direction of their call. When he determined they were but a few yards away, he whistled.

"Who goes there?" David Frisk's familiar voice called out.

"Josiah Tuttle. I am coming in from the southwest." He didn't want some anxious militiaman to take aim.

"Approach."

No one had ever looked so welcome as the dirt-encrusted, weary men from Maple Notch—even the face of Brad Whitson.

"Josiah, what news do you have of the battle?" Mr. Reid came near and looked around him. "I thought Solomon was with you."

The welcome feeling that had enveloped Josiah a moment before fled. "Solomon's dead." The words forced themselves past his teeth.

A harsh murmur spread through the group.

"In battle?" Reid asked.

"What battle?" Josiah asked. "A handful of shots were exchanged, and then St. Clair ordered the troops to withdraw." He made no attempt to hide his bitterness. "We stumbled upon a British scout on our way to the fort. Solomon received a bayonet wound before I could fire."

Around Josiah, the faces of the men hardened. One of their own had died. "How do we reach the troops?" Reid wanted to know.

"We can't. The British lie in between. I considered staying, but someone has to tell my father what happened."

"Don't worry, lad. We'll find a way. We can avoid the fort easily enough."

That much was true. The walls gleamed in the sunshine, much easier to spot than the handful of men who blended in with the trees.

Josiah debated the reversal of his steps as he followed with the militia. With their arrival, he couldn't turn his back. He had written letters home, and someone would see they were delivered. The men wound their way around the bottom of Mount Independence, the site where Josiah had seen the fire burning. Was it only two nights ago? *Could the British still be there?*

A shot rang out. Battle had found Josiah after all.

❧

The Sunday after the militia's departure, Sally and her family attended church in Maple Notch. Even though their itinerant preacher wasn't in town, the Patriot families had decided to gather to pray for the militia as a community. Never had the promise "where two or three are gathered together in my name" meant so much.

But what about the Tories? The thought troubled Sally as she climbed down from the wagon with Stephen's assistance. How could they feel welcome at a church gathering such as this? They probably hadn't been invited. How did Christians with different political views worship together? Both sides believing in the same God, both praying for victory. . . her head swam in confusion. She could almost hear Nathaniel's teasing voice—*Leave the cogitation to the menfolk.* On the other hand, Josiah might listen because of his painful experience within his own family.

When they arrived at the white clapboard church, Sally saw none of the Tory families in attendance. Nearly all the Patriot families had gathered, and Sally remembered Mr. Tuttle's comment that others had moved to town. Was it true?

As soon as they stepped inside the church, Mercy Bailey scuttled in their direction. A warm-hearted soul even if given to a plenteous diet reflected by her girth, she greeted them warmly. "Mistress Reid. I am *so* glad you could make it with your family." She reached into her reticule and pulled out a slim sheet of paper. "Your husband left this with me for you. If you hadn't come today, I would have brought it to the farm."

"Thank you, Mistress Bailey." Ma tucked the letter, unopened, into her pocket and gestured for the children to find their usual bench.

First sight of the letter sent shivers up Sally's spine. Had something happened to Pa? To Nathaniel? Of course not. Pa had written only hours after the last time she had seen him. They hadn't even left town yet. Curiosity plagued her, and she wished she could read the letter for herself.

Elder Cabot walked to the front of the building with the aid of a cane. He moved well for a man missing half a leg. In spite of his three score years and ten, he had a warrior's heart like the psalmist David, and he would have gone with the militia if he could march with the others. Sally was selfishly glad he'd come to speak words of comfort and peace to the families left behind. His daughter came up beside him to move the heavy pulpit Bible in front of him, but he waved her away.

"I am speaking today from Psalm 66, verses 10 and 11: 'For thou, O God, hast proved us: thou hast tried us, as silver is tried. Thou broughtest us into the net; thou laidst affliction upon our loins.'"

The unexpected words sucked the breath out of Sally's body. Where were the verses promising victory from the God of battle and glory who strengthened their arms for war?

Elder Cabot removed his spectacles and rubbed at his

watery eyes before continuing. "Our boys have not fought a battle for many a year. God has spared us. But elsewhere in the Good Book, in Judges, chapter 3, God says, 'Now these are the nations which the Lord left, to prove Israel by them, even as many of Israel as had not known all the wars of Canaan.' He left some nations unsubdued, so that every generation would learn the art of war." Cabot curled all but his index finger toward his hand and pointed at the congregation. "God always tests His people. Sometimes He tests us in illness and hardship as we go about our business. But at this time, He is testing us in war—both the men who are fighting, and those of us left behind." He came out from behind the pulpit and walked down the center aisle, every thump of his wooden leg seeming to count off one member of the militia.

"We have gathered here to pray for the safety of those we hold dear. I challenge you, let us pray rather that when we are tested, we will come forth as pure silver. Even if that means we go through the fire of affliction."

In spite of the July heat and the talk of fire, a chill ran through Sally, as cold as if she had plunged into the river in midwinter. She thought of the letter in Ma's possession, and prayed it didn't portend bad news.

Somewhere behind them, soft sobbing broke out. Hannah Frisk, Sally guessed. She had lost her first husband in the French and Indian War and, of all the people gathered in the church, had the most to dread in this extension of military duty to her second husband.

Satisfied that he had done his duty, Elder Cabot returned to the pulpit and put his spectacles back on. His demeanor returned to that of a harmless schoolmaster. In a less commanding voice, he announced, "I will now read the names of our men who have gone to fight. I will pause after each name, to give us a moment to pray silently." He waved a sheet of paper. "I have written them down in alphabetical order. I don't remember things as well as I once did." A few giggles broke out across the room.

Orderly in this as in all things, Cabot didn't reach Pa or Nathaniel's names until near the end. He skipped right over Josiah and Solomon's names because they had left before the men heard of the battle. Still, Sally said a quiet prayer for their safe return. For Van Dyke, as well. The forest held other dangers than that of the marauding British.

The prayers lasted the better portion of an hour, but not even the youngest children fidgeted in their seats. At length, Cabot read the last names—William and Brad Whitson— and said *amen*. He closed in prayer, focusing on those left behind.

The chill that had pervaded Sally's soul vanished when they threw open the doors and summer sunshine streamed in. On such a beautiful day, she had a hard time believing any harm could befall the militia, and the balmy weather cheered her soul.

Later, after Stephen and Nellie had retired to bed, Sally dared to ask Ma about the letter from Pa. "What did he say?"

Ma took it out. The thin sheet already showed wear and tear from unfolding and refolding. She flattened it and handed it to Sally. " 'Tis nothing private. I'm certain he wants you to see it."

Pa mentioned the rumor that Tories would pressure the families of the Green Mountain Boys who were leaving for Ticonderoga. "But do not fear, beloved. Remember that the psalmist promises that God has given a commandment to save us in our just cause."

Apparently Pa and Elder Cabot disagreed on that point. Sally wanted to believe her father.

The letter continued. "If the pressure mounts, remember the strong habitation that God has provided for us. If you go there, you need not fear any evil."

"He's referring to Psalm 71, of course. It's one of his favorites." Ma tapped the words with her fingers.

Be thou my strong habitation, whereunto I may continually resort: thou hast given commandment to save me; for thou art my rock and my fortress. Sally recited the words to herself.

"And of course we must have faith in God while your father is absent from us." Ma's mouth twisted. "But I sense he is referring to something more." She brushed a weary hand over her forehead. "With this baby and in this heat, my mind doesn't seem to work as well as it used to."

Sally held back a gasp. Ma had birthed two dead infants in addition to her four living children; did she fear what was to come? Surely Pa would return before her time came.

"Does it suggest anything to you?" Ma asked.

Sally yanked her thoughts back from the fearful track they had headed. "A strong habitation. He's built the cabin well and strong, but he can't mean that. We're already here."

"We must pray God will make it clear to us. Now we'd best get to bed or else we won't get any work done in the morning. Away to the loft with you." Ma settled into bed while Sally climbed the ladder.

When Sally blew out her candle, she saw the light of Ma's candle still burning below. Sally prayed that she could help ease the heavy load.

The men of Maple Notch took a different route home than Josiah had taken to the fort, sparing him the reminders of each stop and sight he and Solomon had shared on the trip south. Days and nights blended together, but at last they reached the turnoff for the Reid and Tuttle farms. They had marched since before dawn, and the sun had risen far enough that he could see the river's flow, low enough for him to cross without having to go north to the bridge that spanned the water.

He considered traveling the extra miles with the group to the bridge, in any case. He didn't relish the task that lay before him. But that was the coward's way out, and he was no coward. He turned to Nathaniel. "Shall we go, then?"

Nathaniel followed him blindly, moving in a daze. He went where directed, without apparent thought, ready to jump into a dry creek bed if told to do so. Josiah's sigh offered a prayer to God for strength, and he clasped his hand on his friend's shoulder. "Come, we're nearly home."

They splashed through the water—Josiah straightening Nathaniel when he stumbled over a rock midstream—and climbed out on the other side. The trees thinned, marking the way to the cleared land. The Reids' farmhouse lay no farther than a mile and a half distant. Josiah would rather it were ten miles, a hundred.

"Your mother will have breakfast ready by now. Warm vittles will be welcome." He forced cheer into his voice.

Nathaniel nodded as though it were expected of him but not understanding what had been said.

Josiah feared that he might run into Stephen at work already, but he didn't see the young man in the fields. Well and good. They neared the barn, and Stephen spotted them from where he was putting his tools away. Shouting, he raced to the cabin. Although Josiah couldn't make out the words, the boy's actions betrayed his excitement. Studying the neat, even rows provided a short distraction. Stalks of corn pushed into the air. They should have a good harvest. How had his father's farm fared?

"Ma." Nathaniel spoke for the first time since breakfast. He pointed across the field.

Mrs. Reid had left the cabin and ran toward them. When she saw who was coming, she stopped long enough for her children to join her. Nathaniel picked up speed at the point Josiah would have slowed. Resolute, he shouldered his musket and fell in behind.

"Nathaniel?" Mrs. Reid ran forward and pulled her son into her embrace. "Oh, thank God, thank God." She looked over her shoulder at Nellie, hovering near them. "Don't stand there gawking. Go get your brother some fresh water. He must be thirsty."

Without releasing her son, she turned her blue green eyes so like Sally's on Josiah. "I fear you don't bring good news."

With God's strength, Josiah stilled the trembling that threatened his limbs. "The fort fell to the British." He started with the less devastating news.

Sally looked at him then, her face flushed with the summer's heat, her mobcap on sideways and strands of oak-colored hair tumbling out. Even her worry was alluring. He wanted to erase the tiny lines that formed around her mouth. She stared into the forest, as if willing more men to appear. In no more time than it took to grab eggs from an unsuspecting chicken, she assessed the situation and turned her attention back to Josiah.

"Where is Pa? And Solomon?"

Josiah felt Mrs. Reid's unspoken words. *Don't say it out loud. Don't make it true.*

"Pa's dead." Nathaniel pushed back from Ma. "Everyone else from Maple Notch got away, but they killed Pa." With the spoken words, the malaise that had affected young Reid disappeared for the moment, and he straightened to his full height.

Mrs. Reid wailed, and Nellie spilled water from the well at the sound. Josiah didn't know if he could bear it.

six

Sally's eyes filled with tears at the news, but she sensed Josiah carried a heavier burden. "And Solomon?" She asked in a voice low enough for only him to hear.

"Dead."

Trial by fire. Elder Cabot's warning scorched through her. If this was what it took to become silver—she'd rather remain dross. She didn't bother holding her tears back but let them fall. Ma had her arms around Nathaniel and the younger children. Josiah stood alone with his grief. She reached out to touch him, wishing to comfort him as Ma comforted the others, but she held back. "Oh, Josiah. Thank you for letting us know." She couldn't manage any more.

Although Nathaniel draped a protective arm around the family, he had once again buried his head on Ma's shoulder.

"What—did anything happen to my brother?" Sally worried.

Josiah shook his head. "Shock. It hits some men harder than others."

Although only a year her senior, the weeks away had transformed Josiah into a man full grown. He had shouldered not only his brother's death, but also the task of informing her family about Pa. A man she could depend on to do the right thing, at whatever the cost. Sally wished she could lean on him, but his expression told her he had set his face to return to his father and make that one, final act of contrition. She wanted to tell him she knew how hard that would be, that she would pray for him, but she didn't know how.

They stood in awkward silence for another moment before Josiah cleared his throat. "I must go home before someone else takes the news to Father." He heaved a sigh and seemed to lose six inches of his height.

"My prayers go with you." Sally paused. "Were there any other casualties among our men?"

Josiah shook his head.

Why my father? His brother? But Sally didn't voice her questions aloud.

"I will be back to help in any way I can, as soon as possible."

Oh Lord, help him. Only God could see them both through the hard days ahead.

❧

Josiah wanted to find a route to the farm that didn't retrace steps he had taken a hundred times with Solomon. But whichever way he turned, he found something that reminded him of his brother. That glade was where Solomon had gotten lost as a young boy, crying when at last Josiah had found him and brought him home. Over yonder was a rock where they had skinned Solomon's first deer. That tree marked the end of their races, which Josiah almost always won.

All too soon, he reached the edge of the clearing. Father faced away, checking the progress of the plants on the opposite side of the field. When had he grown old and frail? Or was it Josiah who had aged in the short fortnight of the trip south? A surge of love, of fierce protectiveness, washed over him. He would do whatever it took to care for his parent, even if it meant not fighting for the Patriot cause.

With renewed determination, he took a step forward, then another. Soon he was trotting. Less than half the field remained when Father turned. A wide smile spread across his face, then slowly turned to a thin line, neither smile nor frown.

"Welcome home, son." The embrace Father offered held none of the reservation of his smile. "Did you return Van Dyke safely to his home?"

"In a manner of speaking." Van Dyke had joined St. Clair's troops at the fort before he made it home. "He was well when last I saw him."

Father looked up at Josiah. When had that happened? When had he grown taller than his father? Or had Father shrunk, as sometimes happened in latter years? "Come to the cabin, and tell your mother and me about it at once."

Father didn't say another word and didn't even ask the obvious question—*where is Solomon?* Josiah didn't know if he should be relieved or worried.

"Mother! Our son has come home!" Father bellowed in the farmyard.

Almost at once, the door flung open, and his mother burst through. She ran and flung her arms around Josiah. Then she looked around his girth, to the right and the left, peering across the field. "Where is Solomon?" The panic he had expected from Father came through full force from Mother.

"Let's go inside." He didn't want to talk about Solomon's death in the barnyard as casually as if he were announcing a stranger come to town. He held the door for his parents and followed behind.

"Has Solomon joined up with those rebels, then?" Father sounded resigned. "I feared as much when the militia took off last week." A tired smile welcomed Josiah again. "Although I'm a little surprised that you came back, in that case."

"That's not what happened." Josiah quaked. "Solomon is. . . dead." He brought the word out with difficulty.

Mother's hand shot to her mouth, and she shook her head. "No, no, no!"

Bit by bit, Father pulled every last detail from Josiah. How Solomon had engaged the British sentry, how Josiah had killed the sentry. How he had spent the night at the fort and fought with the Green Mountain Boys, and how Mr. Reid had also died.

"These Patriots and their illusions of independence. It's evil, that's what it is." Father slammed his fist into the table hard enough to send a splinter into his hand. "And now we're the ones suffering for it. At least you had the good sense to come home." He leaned toward his remaining son. "I tell you this much. I know you have a soft spot for the Reid girl. But don't you dare think of helping them out. Or any of those traitors to the king. I had urged moderation in the treatment of those wretched Patriots, but not anymore."

Confusion must have shown on Josiah's face, because Father continued, shouting now. "I won't be satisfied until we chase every one of them off their land and get it back for King George. Including those Reids. And if you set one foot in an enemy's house—don't bother coming home."

After Solomon's death, Josiah would do almost anything his father asked.

Except neglect Sally Reid.

ॐ

How different this was from the homecoming Sally had expected. She thought when the men returned home she would fall asleep as soon as she lay down, at ease now that someone else could carry the burden.

Instead, she lay on her bed, twitching and turning at every sound, every hoot of an owl, every passage of a cloud over the moon. Rather than ease her mind, the return of the militia had multiplied the weight on her shoulders. Pa would never return. And Nathaniel. . .something about her brother had changed. He had taken his bedroll out to the barn, distancing himself physically as he already had mentally.

Without Pa, without Nathaniel, she and Ma were still in charge as much as before. With every passing day, the babe in Ma increased, and her physical exertions grew more limited.

Sally gave up trying to sleep. Instead, she prayed. As always, she started with praising God. The tremendous needs pressing on her fought to gain expression, but Sally wanted to focus first on God. *Almighty Father.* The familiar words stuck in her throat. Almighty? Then why had He allowed Pa and Solomon to die? Father? Then why had He taken her earthly father?

Lord and Savior. Jesus her Savior loved her, and nothing could separate her from that love. Clinging to that hope, she recounted the myriad ways God had shown His care for them that day. From the eggs the chickens laid for breakfast and the milk the cows gave, to a well that didn't grow dry, and even Nathaniel and Josiah's safe return. . . The fact that Pa now waited for them in heaven. At the thought, she buried her face in her pillow to stifle her sobs. As long as Nellie had taken to fall asleep, Sally didn't want her unrest to awaken her sister.

She slipped out of bed and stood by a small hole in the wall, the soft night breeze wafting through her hair. "What shall we do, Father? What if the Tories do come to force us out of our home?" She threw the question up at the sky.

A fierce sense of protectiveness surged through her. She wouldn't let that happen. This land meant everything to Pa, after God and Ma, of course. The land was the reason his grandfather had left England and come to the new world. She wouldn't give it up, not without a fight.

The words of Pa's letter came back to her. *Remember the strong habitation that God has provided for us.* Looking at the night sky stirred a childhood memory. *So that's what Pa was talking about.* In the morning, she would discuss it with Ma.

৶

When Sally woke in the morning, having fallen asleep after her midnight prayer vigil, sun streamed through the rafters. Ma was calling up the ladder. "Sally! Come down!"

Sally slipped on her dress and skipped a rung or two on the way down the ladder. A pang of guilt hit her. She had stayed awake so long worrying about Ma that she had overslept and not helped when morning came. But something more than breakfast troubled Ma; Sally could hear it in her voice.

"Nathaniel has gone." Ma kept her tone even, but her knuckles where she kneaded her apron were pale white.

"He spent the night in the barn." Sally started for the door.

"No. Stephen has already gone out to check." Ma gestured for Sally to sit down and dished out porridge.

Stomach awash with new worries, Sally wasn't hungry, but she did as Ma requested.

Stephen came back in, a few pieces of hay stuck to his clothing, his hair askew. "He's cleared out. But he left this in the saddle bag." He handed over a small square of paper crammed with tiny script. Sally grabbed it from his hands and squinted at the faint letters.

"What does it say?" Ma held aloft the spoon she had

used to dip the porridge, oats ready to drop on the floor. Absentmindedly she put it back in the pot and stirred the mixture.

Sally scanned the document twice. "He says. . . ." She didn't want to say the words aloud, as if speaking them would confirm their reality. "He says he can't stay home and pretend nothing has changed. He wants Pa's death to count for something, and he's gone off to join St. Clair and the troops." She bit her lip to keep from crying. "He's joined the regular army, Ma."

Ma's face crumpled, and she let Stephen lead her to the table. "What will we do now?"

Stephen looked out the open door, as if calculating how he would finish growing the crops by himself. "I figure it's only a matter of time before all the Green Mountain Boys join in the battle. If I was old enough, I'd go, too."

Sally's throat constricted. Every boy old enough to play with toy soldiers dreamed of the day when he could fight in a real battle. But please, not Stephen, too.

"If that happens, the Tories will come back." Ma sounded less certain of herself than before Pa's death had left her in sole charge.

Sally thought of her middle-of-the-night conversation with God. "I think it's time we take Pa's advice. Last night I think I figured out why he mentioned that verse in Psalm 71. Remember that cave near the edge of our property? Over by the river?"

Ma gasped. "The cave. Of course."

"Sure I do. Nathaniel and I stayed there a few times." Stephen dipped a ladle into the water bucket and took a drink.

Sally stared at the man-boy before her. "If the Tories threaten us again, can the family live there?"

Stephen shrugged. "It's not home, but there is space enough for bedrolls and a fire pit. We could bring a few things from here and still be handy to the fields."

"What a wonderful idea!" The prospect of living in dismal, primitive conditions didn't bother Ma. She smiled. "That's it. Of course. Your father and I spent a few nights there after our wedding."

Sally conjured up an image of a wedding night spent in a cave and repressed a shudder.

"The cave will make a fine home. The Tories would have to work hard to catch us there, and we can continue to work the farm." Some of Ma's earlier enthusiasm had returned. The smell of scorched porridge steamed from the pot hanging over the fire, and Ma removed it. "Unless you think we should move into town with the other families." Her voice trailed off.

"Pa would want us to work the land." Sally wondered why she was lecturing her mother on her father's wishes. But Pa *had* asked her to watch out for Ma. "If they threaten us, we can leave the fields that day. But there's nothing to stop us from returning, not as long as we're close by."

"I think she's right, Ma." The challenge had excited Stephen.

"Can you handle the work by yourself, Stephen?"

"I'll help," Sally said.

"Me, too!" Nellie added.

"Very well, then." Determination straightened Ma's spine. "Let's get ready for the cave. Move things a few at a time, so as not to arouse any suspicion." She looked around her kitchen, and Sally saw it with her eyes. The shelf Pa had built to hold a candle and the family Bible. The flour and sugar tins bought from a traveling peddler. The well-crafted oven built into the side of the fireplace. Everything a well-provided cabin could offer. And Sally was asking Ma to give it up to cook over an open fire in a hole in the ground.

Elder Cabot's words came back to her. All of them would have to sacrifice to bring the new republic to life, a birth by fire.

After promising to come back at lunch to carry a few things to the cave, Stephen took Nellie to the barn to choose which tools to move. Sally sat down with Ma and surveyed the kitchen.

"How shall we manage to move it all?" Sally looked at the jars and crocks along the wall.

"We won't. We don't need much. A pan or two. A few staples. We'll live simply." Ma patted Sally's hand. "Thank you for speaking up. You're right: it's what your father would have wanted."

With the decision made, Sally pondered the implications. If they lived in the cave, would anyone know they were there? Should anyone? What if they were still there when the time came for Ma to have her baby?

"I want to tell Josiah." The words popped out of Sally's mouth.

"Josiah Tuttle?" Ma raised her eyebrows. "That we're going to the cave?"

Sally hadn't intended to voice the thought, but it felt right. She nodded.

"I don't think that's wise, dear. Josiah has been a stalwart friend, but he has problems of his own now."

An ache pounded in Sally's heart. She wanted to speak

with Josiah to ease his pain as she shared her own. Of all the people she wouldn't see once they moved, she would miss Josiah most of all. The tears she had held at bay ever since hearing about Pa spilled down her cheeks.

"Oh my dear girl." Ma dabbed at her cheeks with the corner of her apron. "I know, I know. But Ben's been given an awful burden to bear, and he won't look kindly on us, I fear."

That's not right, Sally fumed. *It's not our fault Solomon died.*

But the heart didn't always listen to reason. Even Sally knew that. She drew in a deep breath.

"If he comes looking for us?" Sally voiced her hope aloud.

"Then we'll see."

Sally helped Ma sort through her kitchen things, putting together a small crate with essentials. As she placed a crock of molasses, a tin of flour. . .with each item she packed, she said a prayer.

Oh Lord, let it be. Let it be.

seven

A familiar bobolink call drew Josiah's attention as he walked through the fields. The militia wanted his attention. But Father worked only two rows over. He couldn't slip away undetected.

The dinner bell sounded, solving the problem. Josiah called to Father, "I'll be right there. I think I see a rabbit at the end of the clearing. Perhaps we can have some stew this evening."

Lord, is that a sin? Josiah decided it wasn't. He had seen movement that could be a rabbit, even though he didn't think so. He strolled to the edge of the cultivated area, but as soon as Father went into the house, he sprinted toward the woods.

To his surprise, David Frisk, not Nathaniel Reid, waited for him.

"The Green Mountain Boys are gathering?" Josiah asked.

David nodded. "Allen has called us together. It's time for us to fight the British with the rest of the colonies."

Josiah shifted his feet. A month, even two weeks ago, he wouldn't have hesitated, no matter what Father said. But now, with Solomon's death, everything had changed.

"When?" was all he asked.

"On the morrow. We're joining with groups from Stowe and St. Albans and going to meet Allen." When Josiah didn't reply, David made as if to move. "We'll see you, then, on the green at daybreak. I have others I need to alert."

"Wait a moment." Tomorrow didn't give Josiah much time

to decide. Not that he needed any. No amount of waiting would change the circumstances. "I can't come with you." The words pulled from the depths of Josiah's soul like coal being dragged from the fire in his belly through his throat. "Not with Father so opposed. Not after Solomon's death."

"You're not turning into a Loyalist, are you?" Frisk frowned. "Of course not. You're in a difficult position. We all recognize that. I can't say I'm surprised. Sorry to lose you, though. You're a good man."

A good man. That was a laugh. A man who let his own brother die. "What about Nathaniel Reid? I expected him to bring the news."

"Young Reid? I thought you knew since you're so close. He's already gone." Frisk waved farewell and melted back into the forest.

Josiah's heart followed Frisk's footsteps before he headed back for the cabin. A rabbit did cross his path, and Josiah made a halfhearted effort to catch it before it hid in the tall grass.

So Nathaniel had already joined the battle.

No matter what Father said, Josiah had to visit the Reids.

&

"Now there. This isn't so bad." Ma placed her hands on her hips and relaxed a fraction. They had finished moving the last of their things into the cave.

Sally didn't agree. The cave had seemed spacious enough upon first sight, only a little smaller than their cabin. The problem was that they had twice as much to put in the same amount of space. Without a loft, all four of them would have to sleep in close quarters.

"At least it's summer. We won't need a fire as much." Sally

observed, although she pulled her arms close against the cold.

Ma shook her head. "It won't get much warmer in here. It stays pretty much the same temperature year round. Caves tend to be that way, Don told me." She pointed to the fire pit, a small indentation between the bedrolls. "And I already have a place to cook."

Sally rubbed her elbows. It might work, although the adjustment from midsummer heat to the dank coolness of the cave might bring on a cold. Of course they wouldn't work in the crucible of the daytime. They hoped when the Tories found the abandoned cabin with letters from Ma's family in far away Dover, they would think they had left. Perhaps they would relax when they discovered the Reids weren't at home or in town.

All four of them had spent the last couple of days moving things to the cave, scurrying two at a time, in the predawn hours and again in twilight's fading light. They had brought three of their laying hens with them. Their livestock had given them the greatest concern. If they had truly moved, they would have brought the animals with them. But as things stood, they couldn't sell them or tend to them on a regular basis without alerting the town to their real plans. They let the horses and bulls go to forage in the fields; during the summer, the animals should have plenty. The milk cow required daily attention. They put her in a fenced area near the field.

They considered working during the nights. On evenings when the moon and stars provided sufficient light, they did. But most times they couldn't see with the available nighttime light and didn't want to run the risk of artificial illumination visible from miles away—from the Tuttles' farm, specifically.

The best times to work proved to be predawn and twilight.

They made a quick supper of leftover beans and headed for the field, neglected too long in their haste to move.

"Do we have to?" Nellie covered a yawn with her hand. Poor Nellie. The first night, she had chattered nonstop, talking so much that Sally was afraid her very voice would give them away. Last night, she had drooped a little, and tonight, when they needed her in the fields, she could hardly move.

"I don't wish to leave you here alone." Ma hugged her youngest to her. "But bring your coat with you. If you get too tired, you can use it to cushion your head and take a nap."

Stephen scowled a bit at that announcement—probably wondering why he had to work when Nellie didn't—but Ma's compassionate wisdom impressed Sally as always. She grabbed the hoes waiting by the entrance and stooped to exit the cave.

A couple of hours later, Sally wished she could join Nellie where she lay on the ground. The hoe proved useless, so she dropped it and pulled at the weeds with her hands. *Stop slashing so hard, or you'll pull up the plants by the roots.* She felt so lonely, so cut off from people. Without Pa—Nathaniel—Josiah—and only Ma and her younger brother and sister for company, she could predict how each day would go, how each person would act and what they would say. She missed Josiah more than she thought possible. Until their contact had been cut off, she hadn't realized how much she *counted* on seeing him.

Ever since she was a little girl, Nathaniel would head over to the Tuttle farm to play, or Josiah and Solomon came their way. How she missed those days. Her heart swelled with longing for all of them. Josiah. Nathaniel. Solomon. *Pa.*

Maybe she focused on Josiah's absence because she didn't want to think about Pa's death. She blinked back tears. If Ma, who had loved Pa enough to marry him and was still carrying his child, could keep on working, so could she.

She glanced one row over, where Nellie lay curled up on the ground, shawl tucked around her shoulders. Ma bent over and took the spade from her hands. When she straightened, she put her hand to the small of her back to support her increasing bulk. She saw Sally watching her, and smiled wearily.

"Not much more to do tonight."

Sally looked at her half-finished row. *Move faster*, she scolded herself. She didn't want to hold the family up, to need their help to finish her task so they could all retire for the night.

"It's a mite bit dry." Stephen ran dirt through his fingers. "It would be good if we could water it."

"We can bring water from the river in the morning." Sally glanced at Ma. "Since we only have two yokes, Stephen and I will go. Why don't you stay home with Nellie?"

Home. What a strange word to apply to a cave. By this hour of the night, she was ready to go to their new home, whatever it might be. Sweeping down the rest of her row, she tugged out a handful of weeds, and announced. "There. I'm done." She bent over Nellie and shook her awake. She wished one of them could carry her sister, but the fact of the matter was, not even Stephen was big enough to carry his half-grown sister.

The four of them trudged under the canopy of trees, following a trail that became more defined each day. Perhaps they should change the path they took. If someone came looking for them, they would spot their tracks easily enough. The thought hopped into Sally's mind like a rabbit and then out again. Nellie entered the cave first and lay near the far wall. As the least likely to roll and get hurt, Sally went next, by the fire, with Ma on the opposite side. Musket ready to hand, Stephen slept nearest the entrance. Flames flickered across Ma's tired face, and Sally lifted her up in prayer. She recited her ABCs—*The Lord is almighty. He is blessed. He is compassionate*—before she succumbed to sleep. Predawn hours came early during summer.

When Sally woke the next morning, Ma and Nellie still slept soundly. *And may they stay that way.* Ma needed the rest. Sally scooted around the fire and Ma's sleeping form to join Stephen at the entrance to the cave.

"Good, you're ready." Stephen whispered as he handed her a yoke with two canvas satchels attached. "We need extra time since we're going to the river first." Instead of climbing the slope, he headed down the bank and dipped his first satchel into the water. This summer, he seemed to grow by the day, his legs ever lengthening, making it harder and harder for her to keep pace. But he was right. They needed to get started as soon as possible. If only they could check on their cabin. The militia had only been gone a few days, but had one of the Tory families already taken up habitation in their home? Surely not, for they would have seen the crops growing. She shook her suspicions off and sped her steps.

The river felt cool to the touch, but a sniff of the air promised another heat-laden day. If God didn't send rain soon, they might lose most of the crop regardless of their efforts. All the discomfort and worry of hiding out from the Tories would count for nothing. Stephen finished filling his sacks first and slung the yoke over his shoulders before he helped her balance her yoke. They were fortunate, she knew, to have two yokes for hauling supplies, even if neither was fitted to their size. Pa and Nathaniel had originally used them.

Due to the added weight and the care needed to walk through the forest, they arrived at the clearing later than usual. She hated to think of a return trip if they spilled the precious water. Stephen was starting on his second row by the time she arrived at the edge of the clearing. The corn had grown tall, but not yet tall enough to hide any of them except for Nellie. When she bent low enough to trail some water along the roots, the growing crop hid her form. Darkness was turning to deep lavender in the east. The possibility of discovery always frightened her.

Sally had worked halfway down her first row when Stephen came up beside her. He slid onto the ground and pulled her with him.

"I thought," he panted out in a whisper, "I saw someone at the edge of the field."

"Who?" Sally's worst fears bubbled up in her throat.

"Not sure. Might have been my imagination."

When Sally attempted to get to her knees, Stephen stopped her. "Wait." The whisper sounded as loud as musket fire to her sensitive ears.

Using her arms and legs like a baby, Sally crawled through the dirt to the edge of the field. Long morning shadows should keep her presence hidden. She wiggled to a spot where she could see most of the farmyard, dawn's light revealing the familiar outlines of barn and cabin.

She also saw one familiar outline that had no business

being there. One revealed by the brush of light. Tall, dark-haired, broad-shouldered.

Josiah Tuttle.

❧

Josiah had chosen the early morning hours to visit the Reids' farm in the hopes of deflecting his father's interest in his activities. A promise of a fresh catch of fish gave Josiah the opportunity he needed, and he would go to the river—eventually. First of all, he wanted to check on the Reids. If he were honest with himself, he wanted to check on one Reid in particular. *Sally.*

A cursory glance around the cabin confirmed that the Reids were no longer in residence. A thin layer of dust coated their table, and the family Bible had disappeared. No fire burned on the hearth.

They weren't in town, either. Quite pleased with himself, Father had come back from his most recent trip with tales of all the traitors who had fled to town. But no stories about the Reids. "They've gone to New Hampshire, or so I've heard."

Josiah spotted a letter addressed to Mrs. Reid from a Sarah Huckaby of Dover that confirmed the rumor, but he couldn't bring himself to believe they had left Maple Notch for New Hampshire. Not Mrs. Reid. Not Sally. Vermonters through and through, they would see out the war, no matter what happened—although losing a loved one could change a person, as he knew from personal experience. Look at what had happened to his father. He changed overnight from a compassionate man, even if they disagreed about politics, to a man set on revenge. Perhaps Mr. Reid's death had set Mrs. Reid scurrying for the closest protection she could find.

Josiah swept through the cabin again, seeking some evidence

of where they might have gone. Not only clothes were gone, but also foodstuffs and other necessities. In searching the barn, he found no sign of the expected implements. Did they take their hoes and axes with them to town?

In the yard, he saw numerous signs of absence. Weeds had grown over the kitchen garden, and a plank covered the well, to prevent accidents. He spotted broken blades of tall grass at the border of the clearing and walked through. A few feet ahead, he saw the one thing he didn't expect—a field of standing corn, beans, and squash, with every evidence of tender nurture.

The stalks of corn parted, and two figures emerged from between the rows—Stephen and Sally Reid.

Not in New Hampshire. The thought comforted Josiah at the same time it terrified him. *Here, on the farm.*

When he stared at the beauty with hair the color of oak before him, a lump the size of Rhode Island formed in his throat. He didn't know what to say, if he could say anything. "Sally." Her name squeaked in his effort to get it out of his mouth. "You didn't go." In spite of the mud coating her clothing, she had never looked so beautiful to him. Perhaps he was drawn to the spirit shining from her eyes. This woman never gave up, no matter what. One thing was for certain: the Reids had continued to work their farm.

"Josiah." A sad look splashed across her face. "You didn't go with the Green Mountain Boys."

The disappointment in her voice burned Josiah to the core. *Sally, it's me. Josiah.* He wanted to reassure her, but he didn't. He knew the heavy burden her family carried, and another thought occurred to him. "Daniel Frisk told me Nathaniel went."

"Of course." Stephen was less patient with Josiah than his sister. "Not like *some* people who change their minds when the going gets tough."

"Stephen!" Sally's green eyes flashed with annoyance.

Josiah relaxed a tiny bit. Not everything was lost if she still defended him to her brother.

Stephen harrumphed but quieted. Sally glanced around them. "Did you come alone?"

"Yes, I'm alone." Josiah had endured enough of their doubts. "I came, hoping to find you. You left without a word. You weren't in town. We've been neighbors too long"—*You've been in my heart too deep and too long*—"to leave without saying good-bye."

Sally looked at the ground. When she faced him again, determination gleamed dark green in her eyes. "That might have been true. Before the war came and changed everything."

"Nothing has changed between us." He shook his head, as much to clear his mind of what Father would say if he learned of this conversation, as in denial of Sally's words.

"How can you say that? *Everything's* changed. Your brother's dead. My father's dead. Things will never be the same again."

And my father is one of the people driving you off your land. But Josiah didn't voice that thought. "That's why we need to help each other. We've both experienced a great loss."

"Are you saying you want to help us?" Stephen had heard enough. "Come, Sally. Leave him be. You can't trust him or his father."

Josiah considered ways to convince them of his sincere desire to help. Actions might work where words failed. Without asking permission, he grabbed a canvas satchel of water and walked down the row, tipping a little onto each plant as he passed.

☙

Stephen glared at Josiah and then at his sister. She knew her brother wanted her to reprimand Josiah, to tell him to leave. But pain had filled his voice.

Sally spoke. "We can't go home yet. Not while he's here. If he's truly a danger to us"—her words earned a scowl from Stephen—"he'd follow us to the cave. Is that what you want?"

"Of course not."

Josiah finished the row and headed back across the clearing in the direction of the cabin—and his home.

"What are you doing?" Panic surged through Sally. Was Josiah going back to his farm, satchel in hand as evidence of the Reids' continued presence on the land? She wavered, fighting her instinct to bolt, unwilling to assume the worst.

Josiah stiffened. He set down the satchel and strode down the row until he faced them again. "I'm helping. That's what I'm doing. We haven't seen much rain." He gestured with the satchel. "If you help me, we might finish before the sun comes up."

Without waiting for Stephen's reaction, Sally picked up her other satchel and started down the next row. Stephen hesitated for another moment, then joined in. They didn't speak again until they finished watering the field.

Josiah broke the silence. "Tomorrow morning, I must catch some fish, or Father will begin to question the use of my time. But the day after that. . ." He glanced at Stephen before focusing his warm, brown eyes on Sally. "I'll be back to help as much as I can." He tipped his tricorne and left.

Josiah had said he was coming back.

Sally wasn't sure if the news made her glad—or scared.

eight

"Did you catch any fish?"

Josiah cringed at Father's harsh voice. The sun had already risen by the time of his return. Father had completed all the chores, a job that made him grumpy. "A man expects his son to help around the farm."

Josiah shook his head. "You knew I wouldn't be here this morning."

Father grunted. "And now I suppose you'll be wanting breakfast. Your mother has it waiting for us. Time was that if a man didn't catch food, he didn't eat."

Another one of Father's favorite topics—how much harder life *used* to be for farmers. The colonists had wrested food from the untamed land and the land from the unfriendly Indians and made life, if not easy, more bearable for their sons. They should thank the English kings for making the opportunity possible.

Why couldn't Father see that times had changed? No matter what opportunities the king had provided his subjects in the past, he had pushed the American colonies beyond the breaking point through unfair taxation. Taxation without representation went against law and common sense. All that the Patriots wanted, at least at the beginning, was the same consideration their fellow citizens in Britain enjoyed. But Father and those like him considered the Patriots a bunch of traitorous ingrates.

Josiah knew better than to voice any of those thoughts. Instead, he sniffed the air to draw attention away from his morning's outing. "I do appreciate Mother's cooking. It smells like she's frying bacon."

Father smiled. "And hasty pudding browned in the grease. Come on, lad. Fill up. We have a full day ahead of us."

The men didn't speak much as they ate their breakfast. Afterward, Father took the Bible down and read from Romans 13, with its pointed directive to submit to government. "These Patriots aren't just rebelling against the king; they're rebelling against God's order." Father looked at him, but Josiah kept his gaze straight down, refusing to meet his father's eyes. He didn't want to get into an argument.

"I'm talking to you, son!" Father thundered. Mother made a fluttery motion with her hands that caught the corner of Josiah's eye. Lest he cause her more distress, he looked up at last.

"It says right here, 'If thou do that which is evil, be afraid; for he beareth not the sword in vain.' I'm thinking I've been too soft toward these Patriots. Perhaps the others are right. We should insist they turn over their farms to us in trust for the king."

Josiah bit the inside of his cheek to keep from saying something he might regret.

"They've done evil! They've attacked the king, and they killed *my son*!"

Josiah was certain that Father wouldn't want a reminder that Solomon had died at the hands of a *British* soldier.

"I want to do my part. Tell me, son, what did you see when you passed the Reids' cabin today?"

Panic flooded through Josiah. If Father inspected the

neighboring farm, he would guess the Reids hadn't left the area. The simple fact that the crops were thriving would advertise the fact to a casual observer. Father mustn't go to the farm. A possible solution to his dilemma took shape.

"They're not living there." Josiah spoke the literal truth while he scrambled to see if his idea would work. No objections came to mind. "But they had already planted the crop, and young Stephen tended it well before they moved, from what I've seen." He bit into a crisp slice of bacon and chewed on it. God didn't stay his spirit. "It seems a shame to let the planting go to waste. I'd be willing to work their fields." *Alongside of them, for their benefit,* of course, but he didn't voice those words.

Father stared at him. "You would work the Reids' farm? For me?"

"And for myself." He may not have gone with the Green Mountain Boys to fight, but he could help those who were left behind. He would work harder than he ever had in his life, not for his father's sake, but to help a fellow Patriot—to help *Sally*.

"I don't know." Father frowned, and Josiah held his breath. *Please, don't let him object.*

"I need your help here around our farm." He blinked once. "With Solomon gone. . ."

"I think Josiah's plan is a good one, provided he continues to work with you in our fields." Mother placed fresh hasty pudding on the table. "You mustn't overwork yourself, Mr. Tuttle. The doctor warned you after your illness last year." Dear Mother. She might guess the real reason for Josiah's interest in the Reids' farm, but she hadn't mentioned it. "I'll do whatever I can around the farmyard."

"Very well. As long as you keep up with your work here, I

won't keep my son from earning the right to land of his own."

"I promise. I'll go early or late, but I'll work with you in the fields every day."

Josiah ate with a better appetite. He no longer needed an excuse to travel to the Reids' farm.

❧

"Do you think we'll see him tonight?" The prospect of Josiah's presence had brightened Nellie's day, and she had started for the field eager to begin work.

At least one person in Sally's family shared her happiness at the prospect of seeing Josiah again.

"I hope not," Stephen said.

"Whyever not?" Nellie asked.

"Because his father is a Tory." Stephen made the word sound like the unpardonable sin. "And he didn't go with the Green Mountain Boys."

"But his brother just died," Sally reminded him.

"So did Pa, but that didn't keep Nathaniel at home, did it?" Stephen had raised his voice beyond the whisper they employed on their way to the fields.

"Stop it! All of you!" Ma's voice came at whisper level but with all the intensity of a preacher's oration. "We already laid this to rest. Stephen, we'll welcome his help. On the farm. But we won't let him know where we are living."

She turned her burning eyes, too bright for her wan face, at Sally. "*And* we will take different routes back and forth to the field." A branch reached out and struck Ma in the face before she had a chance to brush it away. Tonight was the first time they had taken this particular route, one that lay through a thicker stand of trees. "Now hush so that we don't give away our presence."

Sally appreciated, welcomed, *wanted* Josiah's help. The past two days had sped by in anticipation of seeing him tonight. But would their friendship alienate Stephen? Why did the war have to come between neighbors? Between family members?

What would Pa have wanted her to do? *Josiah Tuttle's a good man.* His words echoed in her mind. How she wished she could talk things over with Ma. But with everything that had happened—Pa's death, Nathaniel's absence, the coming baby— Sally didn't want to add to her distress more than necessary.

Besides, war was no time to think about love and family.

Sally broke her stride. *Was* that how she thought about Josiah? *Don't be a ninny.* How had she construed his offer to help them with the farm into an offer of courtship? Pulling her attention away from thoughts of Josiah, Sally started moving again.

Nellie fell back and gestured for Sally to bend over. "I like Josiah." She whispered in Sally's ear.

Sally squeezed Nellie's hand in answer but didn't give voice to the words echoing in her own heart.

I like him, too.

Stephen reached the field first, Ma next, while Sally and Nellie brought up the rear. Another time, they might go in two groups. Going through the forest all together as they did, they must sound like a pair of bucks in battle. Sally parted the trees at the edge of the clearing, and her breath caught in her throat.

The early dawn revealed the muscular back of a man already at work on the rows. *Josiah.* He looked so stalwart, so steady— all the things that Stephen longed to be but hadn't yet attained. Why couldn't *he* see the good in his brother's friend? And why did Ma seem so—ambivalent? *Cautious.* That was the better word, and the course Sally had to agree was wise.

Upon their approach, Josiah turned, and Sally thought she caught a smile on his face, although the dark made it hard to tell.

"So you came." Stephen approached the taller man with all the swagger the role thrust upon him demanded.

"I did." Josiah's voice matched the smile spreading across his face.

"Your father?" Ma made it a question.

"Father won't be a problem. I told him I plan on working your farm as my own."

Sally's mouth fell open. Unwilling to give Josiah the satisfaction of seeing her discomfort, she clamped it shut. Did Josiah see helping them as a means to gain their land as his own?

"So he thinks I'm here every day, working the land for the King. . . ."

Are you?

"And he's fine with that, as long I go back and help him with our farm, as well."

Ma nodded, as if she had expected this development. Fury raced through Sally. The first thing Josiah did after discovering their secret was tell his father he would work at their farm every day. What would happen if Mr. Tuttle decided to pay a visit? What then?

If Josiah has already betrayed the working farm to his father, what else might he betray? She couldn't shake the thought. From here on out, she vowed to be careful.

❧

A week later, Sally still hadn't decided whether she could trust Josiah. She jammed her hoe into the dirt with her foot.

Instead of pulling out the weed, she bent the delicate corn stalk in half, and the hoe broke away from the handle from the pressure. Her hand slid down the wood, and a splinter dug into her finger. She lifted it to her mouth and sucked on the blood that trickled out.

Josiah noticed her distress and sprinted through the field to her side. "What happened?"

"I'm not a child. It's only a splinter."

He lifted an eyebrow at the broken implement and fallen plant. But he didn't mention them and instead took her hand in his. "I'll have you know I'm an expert at splinters. Solomon got them all the time."

How could he say Solomon's name so easily? Her family rarely mentioned Pa. The pain was too great.

"This is a pretty big one. Hold your breath. It may hurt as I take it out."

Doing as Josiah suggested didn't ward off the pain, and Sally bit her lower lip to keep from yelping. It left a small, ragged hole, and she sucked on her finger to stop the bleeding. She didn't want to distract the others. She needed to return to work, but how could she without a hoe?

Replacing the hoe would be a problem. They had—used to have—four hoes exactly, one for each of them. An abundance, one for Pa and each of the two boys with a spare. Since everyone had started working the fields, all four had seen constant use.

What could Sally do? The tools to make a new handle had been left in the barn. They couldn't go to town and buy one. Without a hoe, Sally would be about as useful as a dry spring on a hot day.

Pieces in his hands, Josiah looked at her as if reading

her mind. A smile flickered across his face. He pressed the broken ends together before grimacing. "Can't be mended."

She already knew that.

Stephen noticed they had stopped working and came over to check. "What happened?" He scowled at the broken hoe in Josiah's hands.

Upset as Sally was, she couldn't let her brother blame Josiah. "I used it too hard, and it broke apart."

"Gave her a big splinter." Josiah flicked the offending piece on the ground. "She'll need to keep watch that her finger doesn't become infected."

Why was he telling Stephen, as if she couldn't take care of herself?

"We brought a froe with us, but we'll have a hard time finding a suitable log in the dark." Stephen's shoulders slumped. "I guess you could use Nellie's hoe until we make another one. She doesn't get a lot done." He glanced to the spot where his sister poked at weeds between yawns.

All Sally could think about was the hurt Nellie would feel if she took her job away from her. "Or I could use Ma's hoe so she could rest."

"Don't worry about it. I'll get you another one." Josiah flashed a big smile at them. "Tomorrow. The night is full dark. Our time for work is over for the day." He turned his back so he wouldn't see the direction they took to their hiding place.

How could Josiah get them another hoe without giving away their secret to his father? Sally pondered the question of Josiah's loyalty all the way back to the cave, wondering if he watched their every move.

ঽ

Josiah waited until the Reids left the field before he began the journey home. Every day they played the same game. The Reids tarried, not wanting him to see the direction of their abode. In turn, he waited, thinking that his presence in the field would explain any disturbance created by their work. As a consequence, they often worked past the point of safety. He would speak with Sally about that.

No, not Sally. Mrs. Reid or Stephen. Although Sally might listen more readily.

When no further sounds reached Josiah's ears, he allowed himself to scan the forest for any telltale signs of their movements. As usual, he saw none, not so much as a bent stalk. He breathed a sigh of relief and headed toward home.

With any luck, he would catch a few hours of sleep before arising for another day's work. He rubbed his eyes and picked up his pace along the path worn between the two farms over their years as neighbors.

Neighbors. And who is my neighbor? The parable of the Good Samaritan had come to life. Nothing had separated the two families—not until the Continental Congress and the Declaration of Independence. Now Father would no more countenance Josiah helping the Reids, classified as "the enemy," than the Levite had stopped to help the wounded Samaritan. He would pass Josiah, wounded and dying at the side of a mountain road, if he were dressed in a Patriot uniform.

Oh, Lord, heal our families. Our hearts.

To distract himself from those dismal thoughts, Josiah turned his mind to Sally, to the way she held back her tears when he pulled the splinter out of her hand, the smile that played across her face while she hummed to herself and plied the hoe.

The hoe. He couldn't return home with his own implement and pretend it had broken overnight. Even worse to bring back two hoes. Wearily, he retraced his steps back to the Reids' barn and left his own hoe there. Father wouldn't be pleased about his carelessness, but he shouldn't guess that Sally was the one who had broken it, especially not in the dim light of the barn.

Half an hour later, Josiah fell asleep on the hay in his barn, not even bothering to go into the house. He didn't awaken until the rooster announced the dawn on the following morning. *Too late, too late.* Already he heard Father opening the door and pulling a milking stool up to their cow.

Groaning, Josiah wondered what to do. Father thought him gone at this time of day. Should he announce his presence or not?

Father gave a sharp cry. "What's this doing here?" Enough light came through the cracked door to reveal the thin slab of wood in his hands.

The hoe. The thought roused Josiah to action. He made noises suggesting he had only then awakened. "Father! Are you up early?"

"So that's where you are." Father threw the hoe away from the cow and continued working her udders. "I'm not early. You're late. You know that the early bird—"

"Gets the worm. I know."

"Repair that hoe, or you'll be no use to me today." Father crinkled his nose. "And take a few minutes at the pump, for your mother's sake."

At least Father hadn't probed any farther into the matter of the broken hoe, Josiah mused.

"What's this?"

Josiah had given thanks too soon. Father was turning the broken end in his hands. "Looks like blond hair. Not yours." He pulled a strand from the site where the blade met the wood.

Josiah held his breath. Would Father make the connection with the light-haired Reids?

Father pulled his lips together, as if to recall a memory.

Pretending to study the offending hair, Josiah flicked it onto the straw, where it disappeared. "It's silver, Father. We can't see very well in this light. Probably came from your own head."

"Humph." Father finished with the cow. "Take this milk to your mother. I'll see to the chickens."

Josiah sighed. Another threat averted.

Tomorrow he *had* to get up on time. No matter how late the night.

nine

Where is he? Sally's gaze shifted to the far side of the field for the tenth time in as many minutes. The sky had turned from dark blue to pale lavender, with sunrise just over the horizon. Still Josiah hadn't come.

She shook her body to get rid of the mosquitoes that buzzed around her. If only she could get rid of her worries that Josiah might have gone to his father with news about their activities as easily. Her mind drifted along unhealthy paths.

Ma spoke to Nellie for a moment and then joined Sally. "He's probably seeing to the hoe." Ma kept her voice low, so Stephen couldn't hear her words.

That was what Sally feared—that Josiah was showing the broken hoe to his father and—

"Remember the verse your pa gave to us: 'Be thou my strong habitation, whereunto I may continually resort.' I hate to see you fret yourself. Keep resorting to the Lord. He'll keep you safe."

"The same way He kept Pa safe?" Sally wanted to throw the hoe to the ground, but she restrained herself. She didn't want to destroy another one.

"Oh Sally." Ma took her into her arms as if she were a child, even younger than Nellie. "It's all right to cry."

Ma was saying that? Ma, who had added a grave marker out in the field, even though Pa's body had been left back near the fort? Who had prayed at the memorial site, wiped away her tears, and organized their move to the cave as if she had lost a puppy and not her life's mate?

When Ma sobbed, Sally's own tears fell. Their cries twined together, dissolving the hard shell that had formed over Sally's heart. The hoe fell to her feet, a different instrument needed for the softening taking place in her heart. God willing, they would reap these plants, watered with tears of grief and loneliness and fear, with joy, like the psalmist promised.

"What's the matter?"

Stephen spoke, but Nellie was the one tugging at Sally's sleeve. "Are you all right, Ma?"

Ma brushed her hand over her eyes, tears glistening on the dark circles that marked her face these days, and smiled. "We're blessed. Aren't we, Sally?"

For the first time in many weeks, Sally could whole-heartedly agree.

❧

The extra sleep must have done Josiah good. He sped through the day's tasks, so much so that they finished the fieldwork well before supper, and he had time to work on a new handle for the hoe. He wanted it smooth enough so that Sally needn't worry about any more splinters.

Josiah hadn't finished sanding down the handle when Father came out to milk the cow. "Still at it, son? You're whittling it down to nothing. This isn't a fancy walking cane. Come on, now, your mother has supper ready."

No, not a fancy walking cane. But a hoe for someone who deserves wood as smooth as her skin. Many things were beyond Josiah's reach at the moment, but he could at least make Sally a good tool. It was little enough to do, in light of all the things he wanted to make possible for her someday.

Dared he hope? Could he speak of his feelings to her? With the death of her father, and Nathaniel's absence, whom should he ask for permission to court her? Perhaps, as in the break of the colonies from the tradition of English rule, he could break another tradition. When there was no father or elder brother, could he speak with Mrs. Reid? Or even Sally, directly?

As Josiah pounded the handle into place, his chest collapsed in a deep sigh. With Father so dead set against the Patriots, he couldn't ask Sally for anything. His job for now was to honor his father as the Bible commanded—even if his heart broke.

He could at least prove the sincerity of his devotion to Sally. The smooth texture of the hoe handle pleased him as he ran his hands along the length. Good, sturdy wood, well seasoned, should prove less likely to break under hard usage. He set it aside and dipped his hands into the bucket of well water before heading in to supper.

The sun was casting long shadows when they finished their meal. Day by day, the hours of daylight shortened.

"I suppose you'll be heading over to the Reids' tonight." Father shook his head.

"Since I missed this morning. I have double the work to do." He also needed to explain his absence to the Reids.

Father stretched and drank from his mug. "Since we finished early today, perhaps I'll come along. I'd like to lend a hand and see your progress." He beamed as if he had offered his son a finely wrought silver cup.

Josiah's heart twisted. Father was offering a peace branch, but he must refuse it. Danger of discovery lay down that road. "That's not necessary. I over-spoke the amount of work." His mind scrambled for alternatives should Father insist on accompanying him. His eyes rested on a partially assembled chair, a project they had abandoned since Solomon was no longer a presence at the table.

"Mother has been asking your help with fixing things around the cabin, like the chair." Josiah nodded in that direction. "And the step by the front door. We keep avoiding the broken tread, but one of these days we might forget and stumble."

Father looked at the empty place at the table, at the space where Solomon always sat, never remembering to remove his tricorne until reminded, the spot that Mother attempted to fill with fresh flowers and their open Bible.

"It's time." Mother spoke from the counter, where she cleaned off the dishes. "We never know when we might have company."

Father grunted and picked up the chair legs in his hands. "I'll do that, son. But ask if ever you need help. I'll see you get it."

"I'll keep your promise in mind." *But I have all the help I'll ever need—from four determined Patriots.*

❧

Nellie darted back to the cave, delaying their departure another few minutes. Stephen and Ma had already left. Sally suppressed a sigh. She wanted to get to the field, to start work. . .to see if Josiah had come tonight. If her fears of the morning had been for naught.

"Do you think Josiah will be there tonight?" Nellie demanded as they set off through the trees.

"Shh." Sally automatically reproved her sister. "Quiet, remember?"

Nellie looked around them as if to say, *Do you see anybody here to hear us?* "Well, do you?" She lowered her voice to a whisper, but intense enough to startle a partridge perched on the ground into a short flight. Something skittered through the brush underfoot. Sally reminded herself that they didn't want to run into her any more than she wanted to run into them, and she didn't worry about it.

"We won't know until we get there," Sally whispered in a way that modeled how Nellie could lower her voice. Poor Nellie. For an eight-year-old, she had been remarkably patient. Sally remembered her own eight-year-old summer, when she had spent long hours in the sunshine, working with Ma in the kitchen garden and playing hoop ball with Nathaniel and Stephen. They laughed and cried and got brown and healthy, not the pasty sallow color Nellie sported after a month spent in the cave by day, her only hours in fresh air under the moonlight.

Sally searched her mind for something she could do to make this time special for her sister. "Tomorrow I'll make you a new doll. Would you like that?"

"That's *wonderful!*"

Sally's announcement lifted Nellie's spirits, and her voice rose accordingly. Nearby an owl flapped its wings but stayed on its branch. Most of the wildlife seemed to accept the Reids' presence as part of the natural order.

They arrived at the edge of the clearing. Sally paused before entering the open space, searching for the signal the family had arranged to indicate it was safe. The scrap of red wool—from a real Redcoat, back in the days when Pa had fought in the French and Indian War—dangled from the limb of a tree. Sometimes darkness and full foliage made seeing difficult, but tonight she could make it out clearly. She stepped into the clearing.

Josiah must have seen her at the same moment she noticed him, because a smile crossed his face, and he ran in her direction. Sally's heart took flight as the partridge had earlier, and all her pretense of not caring vanished. Her face must have given away her feelings, but she hoped the darkness near the trees would mask it.

"Sally and Josiah. . ." Nellie started a teasing rhyme but had the sense to keep her voice low enough for only her sister to hear. She stuck her tongue out before she raced to where Ma stooped over a plant, pulling weeds around the base.

"I brought your hoe." Josiah offered the repaired item as if it were a prize pair of oxen.

Looking at it closely, Sally marveled at the workmanship. The wood gleamed as if oiled, and she ran her hands along the grain. Even the blade, the portion retained from the old hoe, shone clean, not worn from use. She hefted it in her hand and dipped it to the ground—the right height. Pa had designed the older hoe for a taller person, and at times she had found its use awkward. "It's perfect."

He grinned. "I'm glad you like it."

She slipped the handle back and forth between her hands, admiring the smooth finish. "Is this what kept you this morning?"

As beautiful as the hoe was, Sally would rather have had his company. Anything was preferable to the uncertainty that went through her every time he disappeared in the direction of his family's farm.

"No." Josiah sounded embarrassed. "I fear I overslept. I needed additional time to mend your hoe, and I didn't want to arouse Father's suspicions."

So his absence had been for the sake of their safety, not

against it. She should know by now that she could trust him.

He bent his head over hers, his dark hair blocking out what little light the moon provided, and Sally grew faint. In a low voice, he asked, "Fixing the hoe for you has been my pleasure. Is there anything else you need?"

A dozen things crowded Sally's mind. They needed Pa. They prayed Nathaniel would come home safe and sound of mind and body. She longed for her home in the cabin and had determined to get back there before Ma's time came.

She didn't say any of those things, but only shook her head. "No. Nothing you can help us with. You're already doing so much. Too much. I fear you put yourself at risk on our behalf." Her voice trailed off. She expected Josiah to move away, to return to working, but he paused another moment.

"Next week, weather permitting on Monday evening, I would like to spend a few minutes with you by the trees. If we can share a bite to eat, just you and I."

Sally felt her eyes widen. Their last picnic, on the day the militia had gathered on the green, seemed like a hundred years ago. How innocent their concerns about the Whitsons and the surveyor seemed after all that had passed since.

"You would?" Moonlight picnics? The prospect seemed absolutely frivolous, yet exciting at the same time.

"I asked your mother, and she agreed. What say you?"

"I say. . .I would like that."

Josiah squeezed the tips of her fingers, where she held the hoe, then skipped away to his spot on the row next to Stephen.

Sally flexed her fingers, marveling at the scorching sensation the touch of his hand had given her. With a lighter heart than she had felt in many a day, she dropped the hoe to the dirt and dug at the ever-present weeds.

꒰

Ma did more than agree to the picnic. She insisted Sally wash in the river. They hadn't bathed, any of them, in longer than she could remember.

Sally scrubbed at the dirt caked onto her face and arms and in her hair until the water looked almost as muddy as during spring runoff. Now that the dirt had been washed away, her hair was restored to a golden glow. She wished she had a clean dress to wear, but she satisfied herself with brushing down her second gown. Ma laced the stays, tighter than she had needed when they first moved into the cave. Muscles had formed on her arms after the long hours working in the fields. Thin and muscular, not feminine nor pretty—Sally didn't feel good enough for Josiah.

Then she remembered the hoe, the beautiful, smooth hoe, that Josiah had made specially for her. A thing of beauty, yet fit for the task. Maybe he saw her the same way.

Nellie fiddled with tying a bow at Sally's back. She finished and stared at Sally, her face a mask of concentration with her tongue stuck in her cheek.

Glancing over her shoulder, Sally could make out the tail ends of the bow Nellie had tied. She couldn't see much more over the mass of cloth below her waist. "Thanks, Nellie."

Nellie took out the corncob doll she hadn't let out of her sight since they had fashioned it together. She danced around the cave, singing. "Josiah's courting Sally."

"That's enough!" Ma scolded Nellie and gestured for Sally to sit on a stool beside the fire pit, then combed through her long hair.

"Ouch!"

"Your hair is full of briars and such." Ma tugged gently and

Sally bit her lip. "This is no kind of life for a young woman."

"You said you loved it." Sally reminded Ma. She wiggled her toes in their freedom from shoes, which she would put on as soon as her socks dried by the fire.

"I loved your pa and didn't care where we lived." Ma looped Sally's hair to hang from a knot at the back of her neck. She settled her mobcap over her head, tucking a stray strand of hair under the cloth. "One more thing." She reached into her pocket and pulled out a snowy white handkerchief, with the initial "R" embroidered between an M and a D.

Sally hardly dared touch the fabric, which she recognized as part of Ma's hope chest when she had left New Hampshire behind to go with Pa into the Vermont woods. "I can't take this. It'll be dirty before I even reach the clearing."

Ma curled her fingers over Sally's, pressing the square into her hand. "I have precious little to give you, my daughter. But when I started out on a new life, I had this, and now I want you to have it. To remind you of what can be, what may be, that things will not always be as they are now."

When Sally took the precious cloth, she didn't know what to do with it. Ma must have sensed her confusion because she took it out of Sally's hand, folded it into a small square, and tucked it inside her bodice. "Next to your heart."

All the attentions made Sally feel as transformed as Cinderella on her way to the ball. She only hoped they weren't misreading Josiah's intent. She looked at the floor and spoke her fear. " 'Tis only Josiah. I shouldn't be making such a fuss."

Ma straightened the mobcap on Sally's head, put her hands on either side of her face, and looked her in the eye. "When a young man plans a moonlight picnic with the daughter of his father's sworn enemies, he's serious. Mind you don't play with his affections. If you don't care for him, you must tell him so."

Care for Josiah? As for. . .a husband? "Ma, how do I know?" She felt heat rising in her cheeks, but she had to ask.

"Oh, you'll know. Like I did with your pa." Ma wrapped Sally in a tight embrace. "I think you already do."

⁂

That night, Father dallied over every detail. Josiah wanted to wash and dress for the picnic, but he didn't dare. Such behavior would alert Father that something was afoot. Instead Josiah settled for scrubbing his arms and hands and face more thoroughly than usual before supper. He felt too nervous to eat and worried how to explain his lack of appetite.

His hunger returned full force when he saw the meal Mother had set out. She had outdone herself, with crisp, brown corn bread, savory beans, and milk kept cold in their spring.

He stared at his plate, wishing he could share the bounty with the Reids. Mother noticed his hesitation.

"What's wrong, son? You're not feeling poorly, are you?"

Father looked up. "You've been working hard these past few weeks. Perhaps you shouldn't go tonight."

"I'm fine." Josiah didn't want to give either one of them any reason to suspect anything amiss, so he dug into the beans.

"Are you sure?" Mother asked.

"Leave the boy alone." Father made a dismissive motion with his hand. "He's a grown man. Doesn't need you to tell him when to eat."

Josiah scoured the edge of the plate with his corn bread, but neither parent paid any further attention to how much he ate or didn't. At long last, the meal ended, and Josiah took leave of the table. Mother started to crumble the corn bread into the pig slops. Josiah interrupted her. "Can I have that? For the chickens instead?" He smiled beguilingly.

"I don't see why not." Mother handed it to him. "Here you go."

Josiah broke off some crumbs in the chicken pen, in case Father came looking, but carried the bulk of corn bread tucked underneath his shirt. Ever since the thought of the picnic had occurred to him, he had saved bits of bread and meat and stowed them in the deep well to keep cool. That, plus fresh cream and blueberries, should sweeten Sally's taste buds after days of beans and corn.

In spite of his worries that the meal had delayed him, Josiah arrived at the clearing before the Reids. After checking the perimeter, he dug the red cloth out from underneath the bush where they hid it and hung it on the usual oak. Seeing the rough bark on the tree struck his whimsy, and he dug a spud from his tools. On the back side of the tree, where no one would see unless searching for it, he stripped a small square clear of bark. Exchanging his knife for the spud, he dug the tip into the living wood with slow, laborious strokes. He was putting away his knife when he heard Stephen arrive.

Sally's brother looked Josiah up and down. The young lad had grown after his hard work of the summer. If the war continued, he would want to go the way of his father and brother and join up with the Green Mountain Boys. Josiah's heart ached at the thought of what that additional loss would mean to the Reids.

"You asked to sit with Sally tonight." The statement carried a challenge with it. Josiah reminded himself that he didn't answer to the young man.

"Yes, I plan on a light repast under the stars tonight. I spoke of it with your mother and with Sally last week."

"Treat my sister well. This year has already had its share of burdens." Stephen's smooth chin, still devoid of facial hair, jutted forward, leading his body in an awkward protective stance. Josiah wavered between laughter and liking of the boy so determined to act as his sister's champion.

"I will, Stephen. Speaking of Sally—where is she?"

Stephen let out a snort, half laughter, half disgust. "She's spent the day preening, with Ma and Nellie's help." He drew his lips together. "She wouldn't like me telling you that."

So Sally had spent the daytime hours preparing for this evening, had she? Josiah ran his fingers through his hair before pulling it behind his head. A black ribbon almost the same color as his dark locks kept it in place. Maybe the darkness of the night would hide its filth.

Muffled laughter announced the arrival of the others. *Please, God.* Josiah's heart pounded hard in his chest, wondering, hoping what the night would bring.

Mrs. Reid came first and waved a greeting. Nellie followed, bowing as if a lady-in-waiting to a queen. At last, Sally stepped through the trees. The first star of the night chose that moment to make its appearance, and it directed its light upon Sally's golden head.

She looked as beautiful as an angel sent from heaven descending Jacob's ladder, and Josiah was struck as dumb as all mortals in the presence of the angelic host.

ten

Sally hesitated at the edge of the clearing. First Josiah's face lit up with pleasure, then froze, a silly expression contorting his features. She expected something else, something more... welcoming?

Ma must have sensed the awkwardness between the two young people. She crossed the clearing to where Josiah waited with Stephen. "Good evening to you. God has given us a clear night, like you asked for." Smiling, she handed him a blanket she had carried from the cave. As they had everything else, they had beaten the blanket with brushes, shaking out the worst of the dirt and other debris accumulated over the months.

"Nellie? Why don't we start among the potato patch tonight?" Her voice dropped as the two of them walked away, but she turned a blazing look on Stephen.

He tightened his hold on his hoe. "I'll be working among the turnips, myself."

At last Sally was relatively alone with Josiah. He looked different tonight—he had taken time with his hair. A black ribbon held it in place, away from his face, showing his strong chin to good advantage. Dark stubble darkened his cheeks, but Sally decided she liked it. He looked stalwart, dependable—a formidable foe if challenged in battle.

If he ever moved, that was. He hadn't moved or spoken a word from the moment he had spotted her.

"Shall I put the blanket down here?" Why did he ask her to a picnic, if he didn't intend to speak with her?

Josiah blinked his eyes at her question and came to life. "Yes, this is the perfect spot." He flung the blanket out with a twist of his hand, and it settled on the grass. "I brought a few things. Fresh cream and eggs and butter and some other things I managed to sneak away." He spread out his offerings and blushed, as if ashamed. " 'Tisn't much, but I didn't want to raise Father's suspicions."

Sally thought back again to that picnic on the green when no one cared who brought what food or who shared it. So much had changed. And what about the man sitting across from her? He had changed as well, as had they all—but for the better or worse?

Looking into his dark eyes, she could only believe she liked the changed Josiah better. He was constant in his support of her family. He was here, now, helping them and. . .*courting* her. The thought sent goose bumps up her arms, and she wrapped her arms around her chest.

Josiah spread the food on the blanket, even a few small chunks of corn bread he had carried next to his skin. He offered her the largest piece. "I couldn't think how else to carry it without Father seeing," he apologized.

Sally struggled to keep from laughing and took a bite. "It's delicious. Your mother has always had a light hand with baking."

Before eating, Josiah lifted a hand. "I'll return thanks, shall I?"

Sally nodded.

"Dear Lord and Father of mankind, we thank Thee for the bounty Thou hast provided for us. We thank Thee that we can share it together, at Thy table. And Lord, may there be many more such occasions, when this present conflict is over."

Many more such occasions? Heat warmed her cheeks, and she held up her hands to ward off the thoughts flooding her mind.

Between them, they had more than enough to eat, but Sally wasn't hungry. Josiah's prayer had set her heart all aflutter, and she scarcely tasted the food, even when he dipped a blueberry in fresh cream and handed it to her. She took it between her lips, his fingers brushing her mouth. Closing her eyes, she focused on the flavor of the berry, letting the juice trickle down her throat. When she opened them again, she saw Josiah's laughter-lined face a few inches distance away from hers. He looked so tender, so sweet. . .the berry lodged in her throat. When he offered her another, she shook her head.

Instead, she spread butter and mashed blueberries across a biscuit Ma had baked before offering it to him. "Almost as good as preserves," she said.

He took it from her hands, her fingertips tingling where they touched.

Between them, they finished everything, even the crumbs of corn bread. Josiah laced his hands behind his head and settled back against the tree, his gaze focused on the sky. "It's been too long since I took time to enjoy the sky. 'What is man that thou art mindful of him?' We're so insignificant in light of all of God's creation. Someday the war for independence will be over. America will be a free nation. . . and we'll have to make amends and come together. Patriot and Tory."

"Stephen wouldn't like to hear you say that. He thinks if

Tories want a king so badly, they should return to England or at least make haste to Canada."

Josiah's laugh wasn't pleasant. "He's not the only one who feels that way. Some Tories have done that already, and Father has decided to send Mother across the border. Since we're so close here in Maple Notch, he hopes he can join her there later, when things have settled down." He straightened his back and hugged his knees to his chest. "My point is, this can't last forever." He jumped to his feet and pulled her up alongside of him. "Here. Let me show you something."

He walked into the trees, and Sally wondered why. Did he mean to search for their hiding place? No, she didn't believe that of him. Did he want to get her alone, out of sight of the others? Her heart sped up. Without Pa's protection, she felt vulnerable, uncertain.

Before she could decide, he stopped under the canopy of leaves at the far side of the tree where they hung the red cloth to indicate safe passage. "It's in here."

What could he want to show her in a tree? Curious, Sally stepped forward. She could make out little beyond shades of dark. "What is it?"

"It's on the tree." His voice sounded disappointed. "Can you see anything at all?"

Sally squinted. At first, everything appeared in varying shades of gray, until her sight adjusted and she could see what he was pointing to. Bark had been stripped away from a small square, perhaps five inches across. Pale wood gleamed against the darker trunk.

"Come closer."

As Sally stepped closer to the tree, she could see he had carved something into the wood. He took her hand and placed it on the pale spot. Underneath her fingertips, she felt gouges in the wood.

"Can you tell what I carved?" His breath warmed her neck.

Sally shook her head. "No."

"It's J—" He dipped their hands down, and then made a small loop at the bottom. He lifted her hand to the next shape: a straight line across, intersecting with a vertical line.

"T," she said.

"For Josiah Tuttle." She imagined his mouth curving in a smile.

Two lines crossed in a simple addition sign.

"Esss. . ." He drew the sound out as he slid their fingers around the curves of the letter. "Last of all. R."

JT + SR? *Josiah Tuttle and Sally Reid.* He had carved his heart, his dreams, into the living flesh of the tree. Into an organism that would still be alive in ten years, a hundred years—until after the end of the war. He dreamed of a future—with her. Her heart hammered, making breathing difficult.

"Dare I hope, Sally? That you will consider a future with me?"

"Oh Josiah." Tears clogged her voice. "How can it ever happen?"

❧

Slowly Sally's answer registered in Josiah's consciousness. She hadn't said yes—but she hadn't said no, either.

He wanted to continue standing under the tree, Sally's arm entwined with his while he traced the letters he had carved into the tree. He wanted to kiss that arm, bury his face in her soft flaxen hair, so clean and smelling so sweet, but her answer didn't give him that liberty.

Instead he drew in a deep breath and stepped back and pulled her into the moonlight of the clearing. He satisfied himself with kissing the tips of her fingers. "May I hope for a different answer at a later time?"

Sally hesitated. "Ma said to be honest with you." She smiled, a hint of sadness in her voice. "I can't give you an answer, given the present circumstances. Your father. . ."

Father. Resentment flared in Josiah, hot and fierce. He didn't want to have to wait until war's end to court the woman he loved. "I will honor Father in every way I can, as best I can. But I believe God will change his heart in His time. He must. Otherwise. . ."

"You take a great risk, helping us here."

Josiah hated to see the concern cross Sally's sweet features. "Only God knows how He will work it out. But as long as He is our fortress, we don't have to be afraid."

Josiah spoke the words but felt like a fraud. He had said much the same thing to Solomon before their encounter with the Redcoat. The only shelter God had provided that night had been his brother's body coming between Josiah and the musket ball. That was why he wanted to make a difference. *He* should have died, not Solomon.

"I confess I don't understand God's workings." Sally's soft voice barely penetrated Josiah's hearing. "But Ma says I don't have to understand. I can trust His goodness and His love."

Sally's words reminded him yet again that the Tuttles were not the only family to suffer loss. Solomon's death paled when he remembered that the Reids' husband and provider hadn't returned, either. Not only that, but Nathaniel had reported for battle as well, and they were hiding in some inhospitable place in order to work their farm—a situation his own father had helped create.

Did God feel torn when the twelve tribes quarreled

among themselves? How did Jesus feel when his handpicked disciples argued about who would sit at His right hand? It would take the wisdom of a Solomon to sort this one out. *And Solomon isn't here.* Josiah ran the back of his hand over Sally's soft cheek. "Trust you to remind me about God. You're right. He loved us enough to send His Son to take care of our worst problems. I guess we can both trust Him with our circumstances."

Overhead the moon had risen in the eastern sky, casting a pale light that outlined the figures at work in the field. Sally saw the direction of his gaze and turned away.

"We'd best be getting home before the moon gets any brighter." She flicked a few crumbs off her skirt. "And I didn't do any work this night."

"You did the work of your heart. That's important." Josiah forced a smile. "In the morning, I'll try to get here earlier than usual and put in some extra time."

When Mrs. Reid approached, Josiah folded the blanket and gave it to her.

She accepted it with a smile. "Did all go well?"

Sally colored, but Josiah didn't speak. He hadn't received the answer he had hoped for on this evening.

"Ma, I told him that. . .I wasn't ready." Sally looked ashamed.

"Say no more." The older woman's face sagged, and Josiah sensed her disappointment. "The Teacher himself says there is a time to love and a time to hate. Your time will come." She reached up and brought Josiah's head close to hers so she could speak in his ears. "I know Mr. Reid would approve."

Her kind words touched Josiah, and he rushed to respond. "If there's anything more I can do for you, please let me know."

Mrs. Reid's gaze swept across the well-kept field. "You are doing plenty. God is taking good care of us. And now, we must be leaving."

Josiah watched them, mother and daughter, walking together to the edge of the field. He loved to watch their skirts sway as they walked, to see Sally hold on to her mother, easing her over small clumps of soil. He willed himself to look away, to keep his promise not to seek their place of refuge, not to follow their progress into the woods. His deceitful heart followed them into the trees. He could find their hiding place if the need arose. For now, the less he knew, the safer they would be. If he located their exact abode, he might draw his father and anyone else looking straight to their place of safety.

The moon was fast approaching its zenith. His mind filled with thoughts of Sally—he had tarried longer than he should. Now he must hie home. He checked the ground where they had supped, making sure no evidence remained. He came upon a corncob doll, dirt smeared and worn down. *Nellie's doll.* He frowned at it. What should he do with it? If he left it in the field, anyone who found it would guess it belonged to the girl. But he couldn't take it home nor return it until the morrow. He decided to leave it. No one had checked the fields yet; he would risk one more day.

Josiah's heart sang a love song all the way home, and he fell asleep easily in the hayloft. The next few days fell into an easy rhythm. He awoke early, in the expectation of spending extra time with his lovely Sally. They had much opportunity to talk. The crop was thriving and needed less and less attention. Mrs. Reid shooed them away for a few minutes each day, and even Stephen granted them grudging privacy.

A few weeks later, all of the Reids left early, while Sally stayed behind for a few stolen minutes with Josiah. She could find her way back to the cave blindfolded, if need be, and she treasured this short time with Josiah each evening.

"So why do you think Asher didn't have a captain in David's army?" Sally continued the debate she and Josiah had been having. Why were some of the twelve tribes of Israel mentioned, but other times left out? "Even the Levites had a commander. But not Asher. Did they have something against David?"

Josiah laughed. "I don't know. You'd think Benjamin might hold a grudge, since Saul was their king, but Asher? I don't know." He grew serious. "Maybe they were like the colonies. Each one wanting to do their own thing. Even Vermont has refused to join with the other colonies."

"The Republic of New Connecticut. I know." Sally sighed. "I, for one, think we'll all need to work together if we're going to survive apart from England."

As if punctuating Sally's comment, thunder cracked through the atmosphere. She jumped. A drop of water settled on her nose, then her fingers.

"Rain!" They both yelled as the clouds overhead opened. Had so much time passed, or had the storm come up that quickly?

"I'll see you tomorrow." Sally picked up her hoe.

"Wait." Rain plastered hair to Josiah's face. "You mustn't go under the trees, not while it's storming."

"We're not any safer in the middle of the field. We're the tallest things out here." The corn had grown but still didn't reach beyond Sally's shoulder. "I suppose we could sit among the plants." She looked at her skirt; she would return home covered in mud, but it couldn't be helped.

Josiah didn't speak but took her by the hand into the corn and sat down with her, pulling his jacket over their heads.

Conversation was impossible while thunder crashed in the sky overhead. It followed so close after lightning scorched the sky that Sally felt the heat. She hoped her family had made it back to the cave before the storm started. She never thought she'd long for the cave, but in this weather, she would gladly have taken shelter in it.

Thoughts of her family, the cave, and the warm fire that would dry her when she reached its sanctuary kept her mind away from Josiah. She didn't want to think about him while they huddled under his jacket, so close that their shoulders touched, so near that she inhaled his strong masculine scent with every breath. If she let herself, she would dream of his hand holding hers, his lips seeking hers. . . .

Feeling her cheeks grow warm, she was grateful for the darkness that covered her face. Next to her, Josiah adjusted his position. Did his thoughts run along the same lines?

While she considered that line of questioning, thunder rumbled into the distance, and rain stopped pelting Josiah's jacket, which had grown sodden during the storm. Water ran in rivulets between the rows of corn, but no new rain fell. Josiah stood first and helped her to her feet.

"Be careful at the river." Josiah's mouth twisted, and she guessed he had seen the wariness of her face. "If you cross the river. I only know it lies in that direction." He nodded at the trees where they disappeared every night. "Hasten home to rest. Dawn will be here quickly."

Sally walked to the edge of the field before she turned back to wave good-bye. The hours until morning, when she would see him again, stretched before her as long as a midwinter's night.

➴

Josiah was thankful the storm had ended when it did. Sitting so near to Sally under the blanket, in the dark, had burned through him in ways no Christian man should consider. Those feelings spurred him to action, to fly across the muddy fields. Even so, the time approached the midnight hour before he made it home. He needed a fire to dry his clothes and warm his bones. The night air held a nip, a hint of the approaching fall.

Dare he seek the fire in the cabin? Best not to chance it—he doubted he could enter without awakening Father. Instead he removed his outer garments and draped them over the walls of the stall, where the horse's warm flesh might remove some of the dampness. Burrowing into the hay, he fell into an exhausted sleep and awoke somewhat refreshed in a few hours' time.

His shirt had dried reasonably well, but he still could have wrung enough water from his breeches to irrigate a small garden. He risked lantern light to look for the extra pair they kept in the barn for the dirtiest of jobs. His nose wrinkled at the stench, but at least they were warm and dry. His father's clothes hung a little too large on him, so he belted them tight around his waist.

A shaft of light alerted Josiah to the opening of the barn door. He climbed down the ladder from the loft. Father was examining the still-wet leggings.

"You stayed out in the storm last night?" Father's voice held a hint of disbelief.

"It caught me unaware." He had been too focused on Sally to think about the gathering clouds.

"You should have at least sought shelter in one of the outbuildings. No need to get drenched. I don't want you getting sick at harvesttime."

When the rain came, all Josiah thought about was the need to protect Sally from the elements and the chance to spend a few more minutes with her. "There wasn't time. I hunkered down in the field for safety's sake. The lightning was fierce."

"Humph." Father grabbed the offending clothing. "I'll have your mother work on these today. The rain will be good for the crops. We haven't had enough moisture this summer."

Josiah thought back to the morning he had discovered Sally and Stephen watering their crops and suppressed a smile. He missed part of what Father said.

"I'll see you later, then. Get on with you."

eleven

Once out of Josiah's sight, Sally hastened toward home. The slick grass underfoot slowed her passage, and wet leaves slapped her in the face. When she neared the cave, she heard a sound that sped her steps. *Screams, like someone in pain.*

When she neared the cave, Stephen, face as pale as the moon overhead, stumbled through the opening. He motioned for her to hurry. "It's Ma."

But Ma had said the baby wasn't due for another month. Sally rushed into the cave. Ma lay on the floor, strain pulling the skin of her face taut. An anxious Nellie hovered at her side.

"Do you want a wet cloth, Ma? A stick?" Sally asked. *A knife underneath to cut the pain?* In view of Ma's obvious distress, the old wives' tale didn't seem so foolish, even if all it did was calm her spirits.

Sally knelt by Ma's side and took her hand. Ma exhaled deeply and relaxed a fraction. She kneaded Sally's fingers and reached out to touch her hair. "You were caught in the storm."

"Don't worry about that, Ma. I'm fine. But what happened?" Something must be wrong. Sally had been about the same age as Nellie was now when her sister was born. Joy at having a sister filled her memories of that occasion and not much else. But she had assisted at her mother's last birthing, when the babe was stillborn. *Please God, don't let that happen again.*

"The babe is impatient. Like his brother Nathaniel. The pains started when we returned to the cave." Ma gasped, and the smile fled from her face. She squeezed Sally's fingers and then let go.

"A girl, please God," Sally wanted to distract Ma. "I would like another sister."

Ma shook her head. "I've asked God for a boy. One just like his pa." This time, she didn't hide the grief those words brought. "You don't know how often I have thanked God for this child since your father died."

Tears stung Sally's eyes. "A brother would be fine."

They waited out the next pain. Ma collapsed against the floor, and Nellie looked at them both anxiously. "How long does it take?" she asked.

Sally looked at Ma. "It will be over sometime today."

"Before we go to the fields?"

Did Nellie think Ma would jump up from giving birth and go out to work?

Ma opened her mouth to reply, but Sally spoke first. "I'll take care of it, Ma. You just worry about getting that baby here." She had asked God to let them be home before the baby's birth. Why hadn't He answered? How would they manage? "We'll not be going to the fields today, Nellie. But later, you can fix us breakfast. Do you think you can do that?"

Nellie nodded her head. "But can't Stephen 'n' I work?" Ma's situation must have made her anxious to get away.

"Stephen will go for the midwife." Sally made the decision as she spoke. After the trouble Ma had had with the last birth, Pa had promised she would have a midwife this time. Sally intended to honor that promise, especially in light of the problems Ma was experiencing.

Ma shook her head. "Don't be foolish, Sally." She panted, clenching her daughter's hands tight.

Sally waited until her mother relaxed again. "Pa promised."

"But he's not here, and I am." Ma showed some spirit, and that made Sally glad. "And I don't want to lose everything we've been working for, living in this—hole—by running for help the first time things get tough. I'm fine."

After her refusal to seek help, Ma gained strength. She asked Nellie for some water and called Stephen to hang a blanket. "Go on to the fields as usual. It's better if you're not here. And take Nellie with you."

Sally helped him arrange the blanket and then motioned for him to go outside the cave entrance with her. "I know what Ma said, but I'm asking you to stay close by," she whispered. "If things get worse, I'll send you for the midwife in town. Goodwife Hitchcock. She lives on the green. You know her house?"

He nodded. "But do you think it will come to that?" He sounded like a frightened little boy.

Muffled cries came from the cave. "I don't know. But I recollect things should be farther along than they are."

He dropped into a huddle by the door and drew his arms around his knees. She hated to ask more of him, but she had no one else. "And I need you to do something more for me."

Stephen glanced in the direction of the partition.

"Nothing to do with the birthing. But if you can distract Nellie, that would help tremendously. Read with her, or take her outside, nearby. Best of all if you can help her go back to sleep. You know how easily she gets upset."

Stephen stretched out his right leg. "I can do that." His gaze swept the cave, face twisted in perplexity before he nodded to himself. "Hey, Nellie!" he called out, his voice deepened now and never rising to the telltale squeak that bothered boys turning into men. "I need your help over here." He stood.

Sally passed Nellie at the partition and gave her a hug. "All will be well. Stephen needs your help."

"But Ma—" Nellie's scrunched-up face said it all, her worries, fears, sense of helplessness. They heard Ma's groan from her side of the partition, and Nellie shuddered.

"You can help Ma most by going with Stephen." *And pray for us,* but Sally didn't say that out loud. Nellie already knew to do that, and the admonition rang hollow and might only deepen her fears. They had prayed for Pa and the other Green Mountain Boys, hadn't they, and things hadn't turned out well. Sally forced back the doubt. No need to think bad thoughts while waiting on Ma.

"If you have a chance, get some rest. 'Twill be a long day otherwise. Now, go." She guided her sister toward Stephen before going behind the partition.

The fire lay close to Ma, the low flames dancing on the roof overhead. "Thanks. You've been such a blessing to me." Ma spoke between pains. "I don't know what I would do without you."

"Oh, Ma. I wish there was more I could do." Sally knelt next to her mother and offered her water. There must be some way to make Ma more comfortable. She thought of a book, *Treatise on Midwifery* by a Benjamin Pugh, that Goodwife Hitchcock had lent her. After reading bits of it, she had decided against asking the midwife for permission to accompany her. Now she wished she had paid closer attention.

"I believe I read that midwives sometimes recommend their patients get up and move around."

"Stand up? It takes all my strength just to. . .get through the pains."

Ma looked like she was losing strength while lying there. "Let's try it, Ma. I'll help you." Sally reached down as she would to a fractious child and put Ma's arm over her shoulders, then lifted her to her feet. The roof hung close to their heads, but they could stand upright.

They walked in a tiny circle, cramped by the size of the cave. One lap, two.

"I can't go farther." Ma panted.

"You're doing well. Color is already returning to your face." Sally encouraged her mother to keep going.

"Ah!" Ma bent over double, almost pulling them both to the floor. She clasped her hands about her middle. Once the pain passed, she leaned against the cave wall and blinked at Sally.

"I believe that was easier." She managed a weary smile. When she spoke again, she lowered her voice. "But something isn't right with the baby. I fear a breech delivery."

"But that's. . ." Sally's voice trailed off. She knew little about birthing. From what she had seen of animal births, mothers had the easiest time when the baby slipped out headfirst. "I don't know what to do." For the first time, panic as ponderous as the thunderstorm last night gripped her heart.

"God will see us through, but I might need your help to pull the baby out. When it's time." Ma bent over again as another pain hit.

From the other side of the partition, Sally heard the gentle sound of Stephen's singing and Nellie's soft snore. He had done well to get her to sleep. Should she send for the midwife?

"You can do this." Ma spoke as if she had read her thoughts.

For now, Sally would wait.

&

Josiah trotted to the Reids' field. All the plants had welcomed the night's rain, their leaves stretching for the sun. Things seemed to have shot up by inches since the previous evening. Could the rain have the same effect on him? He felt taller and stronger than he had yesterday, ever since the minutes he had spent with Sally beneath his jacket.

The thought of his beloved sped his progress. He couldn't wait to see her again this morning. Every day his sweet, sweet Sally grew more precious than the day before.

As usual, he arrived at the fields first. He spread out the mud at the spot where he had huddled with Sally, packing it around the corn plants that had shot into the air. A few stalks had fallen on the ground, blown by the wind. Josiah pulled the husk off an ear of corn and checked the kernels. They were already ripe, ready to harvest. As soon as the fields dried, they could work with a will. The rains had encouraged the growth of weeds as well, even more so than the corn. He began pulling them out by the roots, which refused to disappear completely.

His work with the weeds made him think about Jesus' parable about the wheat and the tares. He prayed he wasn't making any mistakes. Which Reid would arrive first today? Would it be Nellie, full of giggles and a happy good morning? Mrs. Reid, more tired and worn-out each day, but with a warm smile and welcome? Stephen, who continued to scowl at him even as he occasionally asked his advice on a farming matter? Or might it be Sally, her shy smile saying all that needed to be expressed between them until they had a chance for words?

Thinking of the Reids, he realized the time had passed for them to arrive. The sun already glimmered behind the mountains with the brilliance of a day after rain. He had expected them to arrive early, eager to work this morning, maybe because of his own excitement singing through his veins.

He finished a second row and heard their old rooster holler, announcing the morning. Josiah frowned, concerned at the Reids' continued absence. But he had promised he wouldn't seek their hiding place, and he wouldn't break his word. Not unless he had proof they were in danger.

After three rows, his earlier excitement had drained away, replaced by worry. Had the storm caused them problems? Perhaps the river had flooded their camp. Were they even now struggling to salvage what they could of their belongings? *Should I go?*

Josiah straightened and stared in the direction of the trees where the family disappeared every night. He could find their hiding place if he wanted to, he was sure of it. What harm could it do? If he started now, he might find them and still get home in time for breakfast. He grabbed his hoe and walked in the direction of the forest.

"It's looking good!"

Josiah stopped still in his tracks.

Father.

&

Ma's pains came close together. The last stillbirth had been nothing like this from what Sally remembered. This was going on long, too long. Each spasm left Ma weaker. If the babe didn't make its entrance soon, Sally feared for Ma's life as well as the baby's. *Oh, Lord, please no. Haven't we been through enough already?*

Ma lay back against the floor, panting after the last battle. Sally eased past the partition and blinked against the dawn light beaming through the entrance. Nellie lay curled in a corner, sound asleep. Stephen sat by the entrance, his eyes closed. They fluttered open at her approach. She motioned for him to go outside.

"Ma?" he asked.

Sally nodded. "Go for the midwife. I've written a letter explaining the situation." She had scrawled a few lines in between times of helping Ma to her feet and getting her around.

"Should I go to the farm, for the horse?"

Sally chewed on her lip, debating. "No. But perhaps you can borrow one in town." After today, they would not be able to keep their presence on the farm a secret. After all their months of work...

"And here. Take this." She handed him a piece of johnny-cake, the last bit of food left from supper. "Godspeed."

Ma cried out, loudly enough so that Nellie stirred under her covers.

"Go! Quickly!"

As Stephen turned to go, they both heard an unexpected noise at the same time—the snap of a twig in the trees beyond the cave entrance. He stared wildly at her and then slipped back into the cave.

Sally stood her ground, straining to distinguish the sounds. The hum of a familiar voice reached her ears, and she relaxed. *Josiah.* She wanted, welcomed, *needed* his help in this emergency.

Stephen reappeared at the entrance, musket in hand. He motioned for her to join him. Ignoring him, she walked toward the noise.

"It's coming from this direction!" someone called.

"Josiah!" The word burst from Sally's lips before she identified the speaker. *Not* Josiah.

twelve

Sally. Relief washed through Josiah at the sound of her voice. The cries of distress didn't come from her.

Just as quickly, panic replaced relief. Any hope he had of keeping the Reids' secret had vanished with that single word.

Surprise and anger played on his father's face. Before he could react further, Josiah plunged through the forest in the direction of Sally's voice. He ran straight and true, following the light trail their feet had made. The sound of his father's footsteps only seconds behind him spurred him on. He burst through the trees at the edge of the river, stopping himself before he plunged into the water.

A few feet away, Sally appeared. He ran to her like a bee to honey, and she collapsed in his arms.

"It's Ma." Sally sobbed the words into Josiah's shirt.

They had no more time before Father found them.

Amazed comprehension grew on Father's face as he took in Sally in Josiah's arms. "Sally Reid?" Disbelief and anger resonated in every syllable of her name.

"You stay away from my sister." Stephen appeared from the darkness near the riverbed. The musket on his shoulder aimed straight at Father. Josiah suspected the only reason he wasn't the target was that Stephen couldn't hit him without endangering Sally.

"Stephen!" Sally slipped out of Josiah's embrace. Immediately, the boy swung the musket in his direction.

126

"Stephen Reid? Is that you?" Father scowled. "So where's Nathaniel then? Or perhaps Mr. Reid has returned from the dead?"

Sally's face blanched at the unkind statement. "Nathaniel has gone with the Green Mountain Boys, as you well know."

"I don't know anything. You're supposed to be long gone to New Hampshire, according to this. . .man here."

Another cry emanated from the darkness behind Stephen, and comprehension dawned on Josiah. *Mrs. Reid.* Panic put color back into Sally's face. The distressed sound, however, didn't stop the force of his father's building fury.

"So this is what you've been doing all summer while you've been pretending to work the Reids' farm?"

Josiah willed himself to stand firm. "I have worked the farm. I just didn't tell you everything."

Father's face grew even redder. "You've been working with these traitors? You're no son of mine." He spat on the ground in front of Josiah and Sally.

"I said stay away." Stephen ground out the words through closed teeth.

Another cry came, louder this time.

"Father." Josiah interposed himself between the weapon and his father. "Mrs. Reid's time has come. I am going to do what I can to help her. Later, you may do what you will with me."

Father released the grip on his hoe. An expression, somewhere betwixt kindness and anger, passed over his features. "Very well, then. I will not bother you on this day." He pointed at Stephen, who hadn't lowered his musket. "But be warned. I have marked this place well in my mind. I will come back tomorrow with others, and I won't guarantee your safety if we find you here." He turned on his heel and headed back into the trees. He paused when he realized Josiah wasn't following him.

"Josiah." His voice held a command.

Josiah didn't budge. He wouldn't. He couldn't. Sally and her family needed him now more than ever.

"Very well. You have made your choice. You know that parable about other people enjoying the fruit of your labor? That's going to happen to you. I'm going to gather the other men of the town, and we're going to reap the corn that is ready for harvest and use it for the good of God and king." He turned about without another word and marched into the dense foliage.

After all his months of hoping, praying, working, and wooing, Josiah was left with this.

No home, no crop, not even a place to lay his head.

ҿ

As soon as Mr. Tuttle disappeared, Sally called to Stephen. "Go! Get the midwife!"

"Wait."

Stephen halted at Josiah's request.

"Go!" Sally repeated. Stephen looked at both of them before speeding into the trees.

Sally glared at Josiah. "Why did you ask him to wait? It may already be too late. I fear for Ma." She stopped her words. Tears would solve nothing at this point in time. She headed for the cave and gathered Nellie in her arms.

Josiah shuffled his feet. "I only wanted to say that this. . . discovery. . .may stir up the Tories. The Patriot families in town should be warned."

"Sally!" Ma's desperate voice called out. Sally bent low at the entrance and whipped around the partition. A small trickle of blood seeped through Ma's bedclothes.

"What's happened?" The sight alarmed Sally. If Ma had started bleeding. . .

Ma's gaze locked with hers, something akin to panic in her eyes, and she grabbed Sally's hand so hard that the feeling went out of her fingers. Another spasm of pain passed through mother to daughter, the tips of Ma's fingernails biting into Sally's flesh. When it passed, the glaze lifted from Ma's eyes, and she became herself again.

"I sent Stephen for the midwife," Sally told her. "It was past time. And I have prepared rags, such as we have, and there is hot water available. And a knife. We are ready for the baby when he arrives."

Ma shook her head. "Don't have much time. I need you to turn the baby."

Turn the baby? Sally envisioned what Ma meant. Did she. . . could she?

Another spasm hit, and Ma's limbs stretched with the effort. Her eyes pleaded with Sally for help. She couldn't say no. She brushed the hair back from Ma's face. "I'll do what I can. Rest when you can. It will be over with soon."

Lord, You created the way we come into this world. I trust You to guide my hands. Her mind steadied, and a plan began to form. She peeked around the blanket.

Josiah sat on the other side, reading the Bible to Nellie and looking so at home that he might have spent the last months living with them.

"I need your help."

Confusion passed over Josiah's features. Asking for a man's assistance, especially someone who wasn't even a family member, was highly unusual. But she had no choice.

"I want you to hold Ma's head and shoulders. You don't have to. . .see anything. But I need you to hold her fast while I work."

Josiah looked at her, his dark eyebrows drawing together in a worried furrow, before he nodded his acceptance of her request.

"I'll help you." Dear Nellie. Sally couldn't accept her sister's offer. The girl grew faint at a splinter; she couldn't witness a birth.

"That's all right. You can help Josiah."

Another pain came, and Sally sped up her arrangements while Ma writhed on the floor. When it ended, Sally lifted the edge of the blanket and tugged Ma's head and shoulders to the other side. "Ma, Josiah came." She'd tell her the rest later—if there was a later. There *had* to be a later. She refused to believe otherwise. "He's going to help us. Grab a hold of his hands, because this may hurt."

Sally looked at her dirt-encrusted hands. The book on midwifery hadn't said anything about clean hands that she could recall, but she didn't like to think about touching the baby after all the places her hands had been that day. So she poured hot water into a pan and scrubbed her hands and arms with soap. The next spasm passed, and she called across the partition. "Are you ready?"

"Yes."

Sally didn't waste any further time. She settled her hands in place, said a brief prayer, and started to work. In between pains she moved the baby's body into the right position. When at last she had finished, Ma screamed one overwhelming cry, and the baby slid out.

Relief flooded through Sally, leaving her weak at the knees.

Thank You, Lord. But her work wasn't done. She cut and tied the cord and rubbed a warm, wet cloth over the tiny squalling infant.

"What is it?" Ma's voice called through the blanket.

"A boy."

"What did you say?" Nellie's voice penetrated the blanket.

"We have a brother!" Joy sang through Sally's heart. "Mr. Donald Allen Reid Jr. Isn't that right, Ma?"

"I want to see my Donny boy."

Sally took a moment to examine the baby. Ten fingers and toes, hair as pale as the silk on an ear of corn, toenails so tiny several of them would fit on a ha'penny—perfect. She wrapped him in a clean cloth and clutched him close before poking her head around the blanket and handing him to her mother. "He's beautiful."

A beatific smile lit Ma's face as she took the baby in her arms. Sweat beaded her brow, the exhaustion of a job well done. No worry bothered her. She kissed the top of Donny's head. "Welcome to the world." She raised her eyes, now at peace, to her daughter. "I couldn't have done it without you."

"I only did what needed doing." Sally didn't want any praise. Anything she had accomplished had been by the grace of God.

"Let me see him." Nellie reached out her arms. Sally showed her how to support his head and handed him over.

Josiah stared at the infant with an amazed expression on his face. "It's a miracle, that's what it is." He reached for the baby's fists, then withdrew his hands.

"Go ahead."

Josiah lay a single finger on the baby's arm, so long that it covered it from elbow to fist. "I haven't seen a newborn.

He's so tiny. A gift from God." He smiled at Ma. "And well named. Your husband must be rejoicing up in heaven, although I know you must wish he were here."

Sally looked at the baby in Ma's arms. One last, final gift, a reminder of Pa's love and faithfulness. How natural Josiah looked with the baby. What a good father he would make one day.

Maybe someday. She caught Josiah looking at her, and she knew the same thoughts ran through his head. Heat flooded her neck, and she turned away.

❧

Josiah tore his eyes away from Sally's. Temptation lay down that path. God willing, the day would come. He looked again at the infant, so precious, so perfect. He marveled again at God's miraculous gifts.

"Let me finish up so we can move this curtain and Ma can get some rest." Sally handed the baby back to Ma and ducked behind the blanket again. Josiah shook himself out of his trance. He had tarried because Sally and Mrs. Reid needed him, but now he must get moving.

"I can't stay." He removed his finger from Donny's arm, and the boy squirmed in Mrs. Reid's arms.

"What's that?" Sally poked her head back out, disappointment flaring in her eyes.

Although he hated to be the cause, he had to act now. He had already delayed longer than he should. "Father wasn't joking when he said he would inform the other Tories about your crops. I have stayed on the fence with him long enough. It is time I take my stand." His jaw clenched as he said the words, but he had determined to see things through this time. "Stephen must be on his way back with the midwife by now. I will meet him and learn if he has warned the families in town. Then I'll decide what to do."

The joy went out of Sally's eyes, joy that the baby's birth had brought only minutes before. "We have to move." Her voice dulled, full of dread. "But Ma..."

"I will do whatever it takes to keep this family safe." As Josiah said the words, he wondered how he could fulfill his promise. He didn't even have his musket with him. "I hope to encourage some of the Patriots to come protect your fields—and your home."

Who, he didn't know. All the men of fighting age had gone with the Green Mountain Boys. But those left behind must see that if they could win the battle for the Reids' farm, all of them could return home.

"Go, and Godspeed." Mrs. Reid held the baby on her shoulder. "We will do what must be done here."

Sally looked so lost that Josiah lost restraint. He kissed her cheek.

Sally clung to him before pushing him away. She spoke softly. "If you see Stephen with the midwife—please ask her to come ahead. Ma had a hard time of it."

Josiah nodded his agreement and left before resolve and common sense departed from him altogether.

❧

"He's a good man." Ma said the words that were pounding through Sally's heart.

"He is." Josiah was good, capable, and strong. She couldn't have done what Ma needed without his steadfast presence, the assurance that come good or ill, he was with her. But now he had left, charging into the face of danger, and she had much to do. What would they do? If they decided to move, how could she get ready in time?

For now, Ma needed rest.

"Let's get you and the baby comfortable." Sally watched baby Donny sleeping, hands curled up against Ma, so peaceful and trusting. If only she trusted God like that. . .

Trust me, child. The Holy Ghost spoke words of peace to her soul. She had made her needs known to the Father, and He would take care of her. She must hold that thought close.

Since both men had left, Sally considered pulling down the curtain partition. She decided to clean first. The mess might disturb Nellie. Their resources were limited, but Sally came up with an idea. "Why don't you put on my nightdress, Ma? Then I can wash yours."

Ma nodded and sat up long enough to remove one and slip on the other. Sally gathered the dirty linens into a bundle. As soon as she could leave the cave, she would rinse them in the river. At last, she took down the blanket and laid it on the ground for Ma.

"Thank you, dear daughter." Ma managed a weary smile. "I believe I will rest for a little while."

Nellie held baby Donnie while Ma settled on the blanket. "He's so *small*." He yawned and closed his eyes, and Nellie laughed. "I love you, baby brother."

Sally expected Ma to fall asleep as soon as she laid down, but she didn't. "Sally?"

"What is it, Ma? Can I get you something?" She offered her some water.

"Not me." Ma smiled and took some of the water. "Although this tastes refreshing. No, I'm concerned about you. You've taken the weight of this whole turn of events on your shoulders."

"Oh, Ma." The baby let out a mewling cry, and Nellie handed him to his mother. "God reminded me I'm no more able to take care of my own needs than little Donny here. I have to trust Him."

"I'm so glad you see that. 'Thou hast given thy commandment to save me.'"

" 'For thou art my rock and my fortress,' " Sally finished quoting the verse with Ma. "I'm asking God to show us where we need to move tonight."

"If we move. I have a feeling we're supposed to stay right here." Ma tucked Donny next to her, and the two of them fell asleep as if things were that simple.

Sally looked about the cave, taking stock of their resources. Was there any hope of staying here? If they did, would they be trapped like a raccoon up a tree?

Had Josiah gone for help as promised?

Sally shook away her doubts. She would trust him. She had to.

All their lives depended on it.

thirteen

Josiah felt like he possessed the hind's feet of scripture as he leapt from stone to stone across the river and climbed the embankment. Trotting, he took the most direct route to town, trusting Stephen had as well. He hoped to run into him escorting the midwife to the cave. Josiah would have sprinted if the distance were not so far. People spoke of Paul Revere's ride on the night before the battles of Lexington and Concord, warning the minutemen of the British approach. But Revere had the advantage of a horse and roads; all Josiah had were his own two feet and the faintest trace of a path.

He swung left and intersected the trodden track that led from the Tuttle and Reid farms into town. Once on the clear path, he gathered speed, no longer worrying about tripping over tree roots or brushing branches out of his face. He took a drink from his skein of water and continued running. He had reached the farthest clearings that constituted the town proper when he spotted Stephen headed in his direction, Goodwife Hutchins following. As well as...

Nathaniel! The sight of his old friend gave impetus to Josiah's tiring legs, and he raced harder. He knew the instant they spotted him. A wide smile broke out on Nathaniel's face, and he pointed in Josiah's direction. The two men embraced for but a second before Nathaniel pulled away. "Ma?"

"You have another brother."

Goodwife Hutchins stopped in her tracks. "She's had

136

the baby, then?" She sounded like she had misgivings about following them into the woods.

"Yes, but Sally—Miss Reid—asked that you come ahead. Mrs. Reid had a difficult time, and we would all appreciate your assistance."

She fiddled with her bag as if that would hold the answers she needed. "Very well. I'll come. If I've said it once, I've said it a dozen times. Babies take no mind of their parents' politics, and they come when they've a mind to. Lead the way. But none of this telling me how to find it on my own. I'm a midwife, not a woodsman."

Nathaniel and Stephen exchanged a look. "I'll meet you at the farm," Stephen said. "After I take the goodwife to Ma." He headed for the cave.

"Have you warned the townspeople?" Josiah wanted to know.

"That the Tories are stirring?" Nathaniel nodded. "They're meeting on the green."

"Have the Green Mountain Boys returned?" Josiah held some slight hope. If they joined in the fight, Sally and her family would be secure.

Nathaniel shook his head. "I realized I had left home precipitously. They allowed me to return home with messages for their families and to make sure Ma was settled." He grimaced. "I'm here for two days, maybe three. They expect me back within the week."

"You arrived in the nick of time." Josiah considered the situation. The green was generally considered neutral ground, but the Tories might see this as an opportunity to nip opposition in the bud—if they knew about it. Then again, they might be meeting at a place of their own, like his father's farm, to decide what action to take against the Reids. "You know the defenses we have here."

"The willing but less than able." Nathaniel nodded. "Elder Cabot, missing his leg from the French and Indian War. . ."

"Mr. Bailey, who can't see past the end of his nose without his spectacles. . ."

"Young boys like Stephen who can't wait to get involved."

The two men looked at each other. Their help lay in men who had stayed behind either because their time to fight had not yet come or because it had long since passed. But no one doubted their courage. They headed for the green.

Perhaps a score of the willing had gathered. They ranged in age from ten-year-old Willie Smith to Elder Cabot. Even a woman stood in their ranks.

Meg Turner saw their surprise. "I can shoot a musket as well as the rest of you. It's time we take a stand for ourselves."

"Tuttle, what are you doing here?" Cabot might be missing a limb, but he hadn't lost any of his peppery spirit.

"I've come to warn you of danger." Josiah spoke forcefully. "I don't know how much young Stephen told you."

"Why should we believe you? Any true Patriot would have gone with the Green Mountain Boys," Cabot said.

A murmur told Josiah others agreed with him.

Nathaniel stepped out from behind Josiah. "I'm here, and I'm a Patriot. I stand with him. You all know the losses our families have suffered. Now listen up. We don't have time to argue among ourselves."

Nathaniel spoke with the confidence of a born leader. Quarreling died down. "Josiah knows what has been happening here better than I do. Pay attention."

Josiah outlined everything that had happened since his

return from Fort Ticonderoga, starting with his work on the Reids' farm. "Now that my father has discovered what I've been doing all these months, he has threatened harm against not only the Reids, but all the Patriots of Maple Notch."

When he determined he had their attention, he struck another blow.

"Mary Reid, left with only her daughter and two young children, found a way to do what all of you wanted to do. She continued working her farm. She was determined not to let the Tories win everything she and Mr. Reid had worked so hard to obtain."

He looked at each of them. "If more of us had done that, perhaps the Tories wouldn't have had such an easy time in Maple Notch. If we had stood our ground. . ." He paused. "Yes, I'm saying *we*. If *I* had taken a stand against my father, perhaps even now you would be gathering food and preparing for your sons and fathers to return home instead of staying in town and wondering how you will feed your families next year."

No one dared look at him, keeping their eyes fixed on the ground. Only Elder Cabot lifted his musket above his shoulder with a shout. "I say we fight them!"

The reaction Josiah hoped for. Needed.

Hiram Bailey, about the same age as Stephen, raised his weapon as well and started chanting. "Fight! Fight! Fight!"

Nathaniel took up the chant, raising his arm with every repetition of the word, gesturing with his musket. Soon every man standing was stomping his foot and calling for battle.

"Then come with me! To my family's farm! We have a chance to round up these Tory troublemakers." Leadership of the group had slipped to Nathaniel, but Josiah gladly gave it over.

As the men ran for the forest, Josiah tapped Nathaniel on the shoulder. "I'm going back to the cave. There's a chance Father will come to force them out. I promised Sally I would protect them." He hated to burden Nathaniel with the possible move his family faced, but he needed to know.

Nathaniel brushed him aside. "We must be on our way. Tell me what happened as we head down the path, since we travel in the same direction." He trotted after the others without another word.

Josiah ran beside him and explained the situation at the cave. "If the midwife says your mother shouldn't be moved, I'm not certain what can be done. It's urgent I remain with them. If any harm comes to your family. . ."

Nathaniel's step hesitated a moment; then he continued his forward motion. "I trust you to do what needs to be done. I think the farm is a greater risk. . .more valuable to the British." He took note of Josiah's lack of weapon. "But you're unarmed! Take my musket."

Josiah wanted to protest. Nathaniel would be foolish to approach a confrontation or attempt to lead men without a firearm.

"I have another." Nathaniel must have sensed his hesitation.

They had reached the point where the paths to the field and the cave diverged. Josiah accepted the musket and sprinted in the direction of Sally and all she held dear. As he ran, he sent up a prayer to the Lord Almighty for His protection on everyone involved in today's confrontations, even the Tories, his father included.

When he arrived at the cave, young Stephen paced outside the entrance, musket in hand, cold determination stamping his young face. When he heard Josiah's movement in the trees, he stiffened and then relaxed when he saw who it was. Surprise replaced the worry on his face.

"Josiah. I expected you to go with the men to the farm."

Josiah shook his head. "I promised Sally I would protect your family. If my father returns. . ."

Stephen's dark expression returned. "Since you showed him the way to our hiding place, you mean?"

Before the argument could escalate to needless anger on both sides, Sally came to the cave entrance. "Josiah! I thought I heard your voice." She ran to him.

Although her mobcap sat askew, her hair fell in tangled ringlets about her head, and exhaustion showed in her face, Josiah didn't care. She had never looked more beautiful to him. He took her in his arms and let her collapse against his chest. For the moment, the nightmarish quality of the preceding twenty-four hours melted away. All that mattered was the woman in his arms and the desire he felt to cherish her and protect her from all harm.

Then reality intruded. The sounds of a baby's cries came from the cave, reminding him of all that was at stake this day.

&

Josiah had returned. Sally didn't want to move from his arms. When he held her, sheltering her, she felt as if she was in God's strong habitation, protected and safe. Reluctantly, she stepped back and straightened the cap on her head as best she could.

"How is the babe? And your mother? What says Goodwife Hutchins?" Josiah's soft voice comforted her as much as his arms had done.

"I can tell ye that for meself." The plump matron looked worn-out. "Things would have gone poorly if Miss Reid here hadn't done what she did. Mother and child are fine, but in need of rest. You can't be moving them, sir, no matter what that rascal father of yours says."

Sally saw Josiah stiffen and hastened to reassure him. "We don't hold you accountable for your father, Josiah."

Goodwife Hutchins snorted. "Never thought I'd live to see the day a man would ask a woman to move when she's lying in. No matter which side of the war they land on. I won't speak for her health if you make her move."

With the midwife's every word, Stephen's scowl deepened, and Josiah drew back into himself. Sally had to intervene before they came to blows or did something else they'd regret.

"We thank you for your services, Goodwife." She opened her money purse.

The midwife waved away the offer. "You did all the work before I ever arrived. I'll not be taking your money."

"Then you'll be on your way?" Sally asked.

Goodwife Hutchins looked aghast. "With the men of the town wandering about like knights looking for battle? I think not. Besides, I want to keep an eye on your mother for a time yet." She tilted her head forward under the low roof and bustled back into the cave, muttering to herself, "They're all daft."

A pained smile had replaced the frown on Josiah's face. "She's an ornery creature; that's what my mother always said. But she's served Maple Notch well ever since people settled here."

"But what about what she said? What are we going to do? If we can't move Ma. . ." Stephen sounded as uncertain as any lad his age would be.

"First, I suggest we go inside the cave. No need to continue our discussion in the open air where everyone can see and hear." Josiah gestured for Sally to go ahead of them. "It offers some shelter."

Sally thought of Ma's need for peace and rest and wished they could remain outside. But Josiah was right; they needed the relative safety of the cave. She reentered the darkness and let her eyes adjust.

Ma was sleeping with baby Donny tucked by her side. She looked so peaceful that Sally almost envied her. Behind her, Stephen knocked over a piece of firewood, which clattered as it hit the ground. The baby's arms flung outward at the sound, and he whimpered softly. Ma stirred, opened her eyes, and she struggled to a sitting position. Sally frowned and then shrugged. Perhaps it was just as well.

Josiah knelt down next to Ma. "May I?" he asked, reaching for the baby.

"Certainly." Ma handed the baby to him.

Some of the weariness that had filled Josiah's features fled, replaced by joy and wonder. "Of all of God's creation, a newborn is the finest." He shifted the baby in his arms, and Donny let out a loud squall. Josiah laughed. "He's a brawny, brave lad. I believe he's saying he wants his mother." As he said the words, he looked at Sally, wonder and questions in his eyes. *Will this day ever come for us?* Then the light disappeared from his eyes, and he turned serious. "Mrs. Reid. I'm glad you're awake. It's best if you're involved in the decision making, since it affects you most of all." He handed the infant back to his mother.

As Josiah explained the situation, different emotions played over Ma's face, emotions that echoed in Sally's own heart:

fear, uncertainty, exhaustion, hope. They listened to all the options without speaking.

"We should—"

Ma lifted a finger, and Stephen fell silent. "Since your father's death, I have asked a man's job of you, and you have done well. But I am the head of this family, and I will make this decision." She softened her statement with her next words. "Although I value your opinion—all of you. But right now, let me think."

They could have heard grass grow in the silence that settled on the cave, broken by an occasional mewling sound from the baby. Even Nellie didn't move from her spot beside the fire.

"You say the Patriots hope to not only protect our farm but also round up the Tories who have been plaguing their families?"

Josiah hesitated. "They have built up their anger and want to take action. They're tired of being pushed around."

"And the Tories want to make an example of my family and farm to show the Patriots they mean what they say?"

Josiah paused longer this time. He hung his head. "That's what my father threatened to do."

"Your *father*." Ma emphasized the word. "You owe him more than a date with death. My son, your father, and every other man young or old left in Maple Notch are gathering in our fields to fight. People will die this evening if someone doesn't do something to stop them."

Hearing it stated like that, Sally felt even worse about the upcoming confrontation. She looked at Josiah, at the deep, dark hurt in his eyes.

"Dear Josiah. I've known you since you were the size of

little Donny here." Ma held the baby against her chest. "I love you as if you were my own. You can't let this happen."

"But what can I do?" The anguish in Josiah's voice was painful to hear.

"Go to your father." Ma looked surprised he had to ask. "Sally, I think it best if you go with him. Remind him of the long years of friendship that lie between our families."

Startled, Sally looked from Ma to Josiah and back again.

"Mrs. Reid, no." Josiah stood.

Donny let out a cry, and Ma shushed Josiah's protest. "Your father will hesitate to commit violence in the presence of a woman. He will gain some time to react with reason and not from anger." She smiled confidently. "I trust you with her safety."

"But who will protect you, Ma?" Sally asked.

" 'The Lord is my rock and my fortress.' And Stephen will be with us."

Stephen bit his lip. He probably wished he could go fight, take his place among the men. Ma reached out a hand and touched his shoulder. "Stephen, you'll have the most important job of all. . .protecting me and the baby."

He straightened his shoulders and puffed out his chest, grown broad over the summer's work.

Sally scrambled for alternatives and found none. Ma was right, and they had no time to waste. "Josiah, let's get going if we're going to stop your father before a quarrel breaks out."

Josiah grabbed his musket and headed for the cave entrance. "If it's not already too late."

Sally looked around the cave for something she could use as a weapon. The only possibility was the hoe Josiah had so lovingly crafted. *Don't be a dunce.* How could she convince

Mr. Tuttle she came in peace if she arrived bearing arms? *I'll be wearing the armor of God,* she reminded herself. She had the best protection of all: the breastplate of righteousness, the shield of faith, and feet shod with the gospel of peace. Saying a prayer for the Lord's help, she followed Josiah into the thicket of trees.

"We'll pass close to your farm on the way to my family's cabin," Josiah remarked. "Pray we don't hear gunfire." His lips twisted in what was supposed to pass for a smile. "We'll move slowly and surely. There is no need to run like wild things and announce our presence."

A squirrel jumped from a tree branch, and it swung through the air with a snapping sound. Sally jumped. *The gospel of peace,* she continued praying. The American colonies wouldn't win freedom without bloodshed. *Including Pa's.* But not today, not between neighbors and friends and family. Not on account of her family, and not while she could do something to stop it.

The sound of the squirrel also caught Josiah unaware, and he put his finger into the air for a warning signal and stopped. After a pause, he started walking again. He spoke in a low voice. "The folks from town took the main road, but I don't know which way the Tories are coming. They might shoot before thinking. Follow my lead."

Sally nodded, fear screaming down her legs that she should run, fast. The noise of her heavy skirts as they dragged through the trees made her doubt their plan of action. Without her along, Josiah could move quickly and quietly. *But Mr. Tuttle might listen to me when he won't listen to his son,* she reminded herself. She lifted the edges of her skirt and walked as softly as she could manage.

Josiah detoured on a route that bypassed the Reids' field. Sally wondered why until she determined he was heading straight for his farm. Perhaps they would avoid both militia and king's men and accomplish their task. She hoped God would speed their steps so they could arrive before the gathering and speak sense to Mr. Tuttle.

Josiah stopped so abruptly that Sally put out her hand to prevent herself from running into his back. He examined the leaves and branches around them without speaking.

"What is it?" Sally whispered.

He whirled around, his attitude making the act more threat than comfort. "Someone's already been this way, heading to the farm. I don't know what we'll find there." Without warning, he set off again, leaving Sally to catch up. Given his state of mind, she wasn't sure if he was ready to listen to reason any more than his father was. She prayed for all of them as she followed Josiah's footsteps.

As they progressed, she could see signs of the passage of a number of men, although they had not yet seen or heard them. At last she heard a faint groaning from beyond the next copse of trees. The sound of an animal in pain, or someone injured. . .dying. *We're too late.*

fourteen

Josiah looked into Sally's eyes, questioning pools of pale blue-green, and suspected she saw the same question in his own eyes. Who, or what, had they heard? If human, there could only be one man; more would make a greater amount of noise. Unless the Tories were aware of their approach and someone had faked an injury, hoping to lure them to a surprise attack. He gripped his musket and signaled for Sally to wait while he took a few cautious steps forward.

When he saw the man sprawled on the ground, he sprinted forward.

"Father!" His voice rang out like a bird's call, loud and clear. Heedless of the danger, he plunged through the growth, dropped to his knees, and set the musket down. Father lay on the ground unmoving, eyes staring straight ahead without blinking. Josiah's heart jumped into his throat, cutting off his breath. The doctor had warned his father about controlling his anger and his too-rich diet. Had the confrontation between father and son on the previous day brought this on? Josiah felt more guilty and torn than ever.

Behind him, he heard Sally gasp. "Is he. . .dead?" Her voice sounded faint and far away, or perhaps his sense of hearing had dulled.

Josiah took Father's wrist in his hand and felt for a pulse. For a long, tense moment, he couldn't find it. Then he felt it, a slow, almost imperceptible beat, a rhythm that made his

148

heart sing more than any hymn of praise.

"He's alive." Tears coated his voice, but Josiah didn't care. "Praise the Lord. He's alive." The last words came through a choked throat.

"Amen." Sally's heartfelt agreement rang in his heart. She knelt next to Josiah. "Praise God from whom all blessings flow." The words lifted from her lips like an offering to the Almighty, and Josiah joined her in singing. "Praise Him, all creatures here below." Birds swooped in front of them, adding their cries and calls to the song of thanksgiving.

Josiah broke from the reverie, remembering where they were and why they were there. "If anyone was looking for us. . ." He attempted to swallow a bitter laugh without success. "We've just given them directions."

Beads of sweat dotted his father's brow, as if he had been working in the fields during the height of summer instead of walking through the forest on a cool autumn day. It looked like several people had come this way. If so, why had they left him behind? With the doxology, Josiah and Sally had announced their presence. The others could return at any second.

"We need to get out of here." What had he heard the doctor say about apoplexy? Was there a certain way they should position the body? He couldn't worry about that. He slung his father's body over his left shoulder and lurched to his feet. The weight made him stumble. *Lord, give me strength.*

Two strides later, he paused. "Where should we go?"

"Our cabin is closest." Sally took off in that direction without waiting for his reply.

"But. . ." The protest died on his lips. Here or there, it

didn't matter as long they got moving. He shifted his father's weight and lumbered down the path behind her.

❧

Mr. Tuttle was ill, perhaps to death. Sally couldn't believe it. Whatever animosity she had felt toward Josiah's father for his opposition to her family and the other Patriots fled in the face of the apoplectic fit. She didn't want him to die.

She swerved from her course to intersect the path between the two farms. Speed mattered more than staying hidden. As she raced down the trail, she saw signs of recent passage—many feet. Her heart palpitated, but she kept pushing onward. No one they encountered would harm a woman and a sick man, not their neighbors, people she had known all her life.

Then why have we been living in a cave these past few months? Why have we been farming by dark? Because everything had changed. Freedom would come at a high price. In her heart of hearts, did she believe it was worth the cost?

Josiah panted behind her. His father must outweigh him by several pounds. How he managed to carry him at all amazed her. When she glanced back to see if she could help in any way, she noticed he wasn't carrying the musket.

Fear flared in Sally's heart. She lifted her skirts and prepared to race even faster for the cabin; then she halted. The cabin offered little protection and no weapons, not even the hoe she had disdained in the cave. No protection but the armor of God, she reminded herself. That would be enough. It would have to be.

"What's wrong?" Josiah pulled even with her.

"The musket." Fear must have shown in her eyes. "You left it back in the thicket."

His mouth opened and closed, not finding any words sufficient for the situation they found themselves in. This close, she could hear the thready sound of Mr. Tuttle's breathing. He needed a bed and quiet, as soon as possible. Only one possibility came to mind.

"You go ahead to the cabin." She took a deep breath. "I'll go back for the musket." She didn't wait for the protest she was sure would come, but lifted her skirts well above her ankles and raced—their lives depended on it.

❧

Josiah wanted to toss his father on the ground and run after Sally. Of all the foolish, idiotic things he had ever done. . . and Sally's rash decision to rush into danger. But he had no choice in the matter. He had to render care to his father, and the cabin was only a short distance away. He said a quick prayer as he started in the direction of the Reids' property.

It's your own fault, he reminded himself. If he hadn't left the weapon behind. . .

He called himself every name in the book and made up a few more. The name-calling couldn't keep his mind off the danger to which Sally raced. *Will the Tories find her? If they do, what will they do to her?* He tore his mind away from the images that flooded his mind and went back to inventive self-flagellation. *You're more selfish than the Levite that passed by the Samaritan, you oaf.*

He reached the edge of the clearing and stopped before walking into the open. Anyone nearby would have heard his approach, but he didn't need to walk into an ambush. He gave the bobolink call in case Nathaniel and the others had come to the farm. No response. No sounds intruded on the silence. He moved forward, the weight of his father pressing upon his back and threatening to slip off if his balance shifted by so much as a pennyweight. At the door, he used its surface to prop up Father's body while he turned the knob. It sprang open, and Josiah caught his father just in time before he fell onto the floor.

The soft tick bed beckoned from the corner, and Josiah laid down his father's body. How much harm had the run through the forest caused? Panic set in when he had to press his fingers hard for a pulse. Finding it at last, he sagged over his father's body.

What had the doctor said after Father's last attack? Did he need to be warmer or cooler? Would a blistering plaster help or harm? Not that he could find the ingredients for a plaster in the kitchen—the Reids had emptied it out when they moved—or that he would know how to make it. Such knowledge usually resided with the women of the family, but they were in Canada. The doctor's instructions were at his family's cabin. Maybe he should have taken Father there, after all. He did remember the doctor had said to call him to bleed the patient.

But Josiah was here, in the deserted home of the Reids, while the doctor, a Patriot, was away fighting with the Green Mountain Boys, without any herbal remedies available. What else could have the doctor suggested? *Raise Father's head.* He could do that much. Loosen his clothes and keep him cool—now he remembered—so no blanket.

Sally should be here by now. After he had done what he could without more supplies or the doctor, Josiah paced the cabin and wondered when she would arrive. Why, oh why, had he forgotten the musket? Why had he allowed her to go back after it? Why had God allowed his father's apoplexy and the threat to all their lives to happen at the same time?

No answer came. He knew it was foolish to think about it; wondering why wouldn't change a thing. Perhaps now that Father was settled, Josiah could chance going back to escort Sally to the cabin.

"Tuttle, we know you're in there."

Josiah recognized Hawkins, one of the Tory leaders.

"We have something you want."

Dread seized Josiah, and he flung the door open.

Hawkins held Sally close, his arm hugging her neck, knife to her throat.

ॐ

"Josiah." Sally couldn't keep the quiver from her voice, in spite of her best efforts. Because of her failure to retrieve the musket in time, they were in more danger than ever.

"Josiah, is it?" Hawkins imitated her voice, making her sound like a helpless maiden without a knight to come to her rescue. He pressed the knife tip into her skin, and she flinched.

Josiah took a step forward.

"Stop there, Tuttle. Come any closer and. . ."

Sally felt the knife cross her throat, a whisker's breadth from her skin.

Josiah stopped moving.

A foul stench invaded Sally's nostrils when next Hawkins spoke. "It seems like you and 'Miss Reid' have become good friends, very good friends indeed. To think that all this time you've been pretending to be such a good son to your father."

Had her single, involuntary cry of Josiah's name put them in even greater danger? She pled for forgiveness with her eyes. She dared not speak again.

"Hawkins." Josiah held his position and extended his arms in front of him, showing them all he had no weapon.

My fault, all my fault. Sally moaned, and Hawkins put his hard hand over her mouth. "No noise making."

"You're not thinking clearly," Josiah said, not moving from his spot.

"What? Because I believe God's command to honor the king?"

Sally didn't believe even the hated King George would approve of Hawkins's actions on this day.

"Because the Hawkins I know wouldn't harm innocent people. Women, children—sick men like my father."

"Your father is the reason we're here. Some in the group said how we ought to go back and check on him, it wasn't right to leave him there. And that's when we found Miss Reid here, retrieving the musket." He brandished it with his left hand.

Coming from Hawkins's mouth, *Miss Reid* sounded like a curse. Sally forced herself not to shiver.

"If you believed in the king's cause, you'd have joined General Burgoyne in his campaign." Josiah seemed to be sneering at Hawkins. "Real men fight real battles. They don't pick on women and children." His eyes focused on Sally, willing her to some action that she couldn't determine.

"Why, you—"

"Afraid to fight like a man?" No doubt about it, Josiah was taunting the Tory.

"I'm not afraid of you." Hawkins dragged Sally forward a few inches, thrusting his knife in Josiah's direction.

"Not willing to fight on equal terms, no weapons, hand to hand, one on one?"

Hawkins moved forward until Josiah was only inches away. "I'm ready whenever you are."

Josiah cocked his fists but spoke to the gathering. "Promise me you won't let your men run like wild things if things go poorly for you?"

Josiah glanced at Sally and then at the woods. Sally thought back to Josiah's warning as they walked through the forest. *Does he mean. . . ?*

"Or will they run away like scared rabbits?" When he looked at her this time, she was certain she understood his meaning.

"Don't know why I should promise anything to a rebel like you." Hawkins shoved Sally aside.

She lifted her skirts and fled in the direction of the forest, where she knew every tree and leaf and hollow. If she could get away, she could go to Nathaniel and the other Patriots for help. *Lord, please, please protect Josiah.* Brambles tore her skirt and left scratches on her ankles as she headed into the woods. As soon as she judged it was safe, she circled back to the fields.

A shape loomed in front of her, gripping her shoulders, and clapped a hand over her mouth before her scream could escape. She saw it was Nathaniel and relaxed.

"Why are you running through the woods like a deer escaping a hunter?" He asked.

"They have Josiah." She paused, taking a deep gulp of air. "At our cabin."

Nathaniel gestured, and for the first time, Sally noticed the others gathered around him. "They took the battle to the cabin instead of to the fields," he said. "Let's go."

They fled into the trees before Sally caught her breath and

could move again. Elder Cabot hobbled up to her, making surprising speed with his wooden leg. "Would you keep an old man company and see what we can do to help?"

"Of course." She took the man's arm, his other hand holding on to a cane, and they followed behind. Now that she was no longer running, the scratches on her legs began to burn. She focused on listening for gunfire.

A single shot rang out, and both of them picked up speed. They arrived at the clearing only a couple of minutes behind Nathaniel and the others, but the sight that greeted them brought tears to Sally's eyes. Each Patriot had a Tory at gunpoint. Smoke curled from the end of Meg Turner's musket. She must have fired a warning shot.

Only Josiah and Hawkins continued to fight, hand to hand, as promised.

They looked like death alone would stop the combat.

fifteen

Josiah had heard Nathaniel's call, the warning shot, the thud of weapons dropping on the ground. But he didn't let any of the action distract his attention from Hawkins.

Hawkins, however, looked at the commotion. Only for a moment, but that was long enough for Josiah to land a solid punch on his jaw that sent him staggering back. "That one's for Sally. For threatening her." He said it so low that he doubted anyone heard it in the general melee.

Hawkins's eyes narrowed, and he tried a counterpunch that Josiah easily dodged. "Your help has arrived." He sneered.

Josiah darted in long enough to land a couple of blows on Hawkins's exposed abdomen. "And *that's* for calling me a coward."

Hawkins doubled over, but Josiah didn't slow down. He rained blows on his head. "And that's for leaving my father to die in the woods."

Hawkins moaned.

"Josiah! Stop!" Sally's gentle voice penetrated the angry fog created by the months of grief and alienation that had swarmed around him. The red haze cleared from his vision, and he looked at Hawkins with amazement. The man lay prone on the ground. Sally didn't pay attention to his injuries, however. She dipped a rag in a bucket of water from the well and held it up to Josiah's face. It came away smeared with mud and blood.

The touch stung, but he wouldn't have stopped Sally's ministrations for anything.

"You're hurt."

"Time will heal me. But—"

"I'm so sorry. If I hadn't let them catch me. . ."

"I'm the fool for leaving the musket behind."

"Shh." She wrung out the rag and ran it over his face one more time. "Your father? Is he. . . ?"

Father! How could Josiah have forgotten him in the midst of the fight? "He was still breathing when Hawkins and the others arrived." He wiped his hands—covered with Hawkins's blood—on the rag and walked for the door. Sally followed.

Father was breathing heavily, noisily. Never had his labored breathing sounded so sweet, since only an hour earlier the breath of life fluttered silently within him, almost nonexistent. Josiah flung himself by his father's side

"You're alive!"

Father's eyelids fluttered open, and dark eyes glared at Josiah. "I should hope so." He lifted his head a quarter of an inch, dropped it back against the pillow, and grunted. "Where am I?"

"You're in our cabin, Mr. Tuttle." Sally knelt by his other side. "Praise God you've awakened. You gave us a fright."

"Get me"—Father made an effort in earnest to sit up before he sank back against the tick—"out of here."

"You're not going anywhere." Josiah could bark as well as his father.

Sally threw a reproachful look his way before she put a soothing hand on the old man's brow. "We found you in the forest and brought you here since it was closest."

"I'd rather—"

Sally rode over his protest. "Now rest. All this fuss can do you no good."

"Josiah." Nathaniel had entered the cabin.

Sally lifted a finger to her mouth and gestured for the two men to go outside. Josiah spared a glance at his father, debating whether the man would give Sally a hard time, and decided no, he wouldn't. Besides, Father had already closed his eyes again. Josiah stepped outside with Nathaniel.

"We got fourteen of 'em. Fifteen, if we count your father." Nathaniel spoke with all the excitement of a newly minted commander.

The Tory men stood in a circle, rope tied betwixt and around them. Josiah was relieved to see Hawkins on his feet. "So I see. What are you going to do with them?"

"String 'em up!" That cry came from one of the young boys, hotheaded and eager for battle. "For being traitors to their country."

Hawkins straightened his shoulders and glared at Josiah from underneath swelling eyelids. "It's you who are the traitors. You can kill us if you like, but your time will come."

Josiah had to admire Hawkins's courage. He started to speak but stopped himself. Because of his father, any pleas he made on the Tories' behalf might do more harm than good. Instead he looked at his friend. "What does Nathaniel think?"

"I have no use for the lot of them or their cause." Nathaniel paced around the circle of captured men. "But they're our neighbors. We used to call them our friends. We've worshipped together."

"Too scared to kill us?" Hawkins taunted.

Be quiet, fool. Hawkins's outburst frustrated and frightened Josiah.

Nathaniel drew a deep breath. "I say we lock them up until we can hand them over to Major General St. Clair. Let them face military justice. We can set up shifts guarding the gaol until then."

"Confiscate their property!" one of the young bucks called.

"No, son." Cabot hobbled to the front. "The Good Book says to do to others as we want them to do to us. Not like they treat us. We are the better men and should leave their families in peace. Let St. Clair deal with them and make the decisions."

A murmur of agreement spread through the crowd at Cabot's words of wisdom, and Josiah relaxed. The meeting broke up as the men decided how to get the prisoners into town.

"For a moment there"—Josiah looked at Nathaniel—"I was afraid you'd have a mutiny on your hands."

"Me, too." Nathaniel shook his head. "I've had enough fighting without engaging people I've known my whole life. Now tell me about your father."

Josiah explained about the apoplexy and the doctor's warnings after his father's illness last year. "There's not much more we can do now, since the doctor went off with the Green Mountain Boys. Sally offered your cabin."

"Of course. Leastwise until we get Ma back. I'm going over there to check on her now." He glanced at the sky to gauge the time of day. "Looks like we've still got some daylight left. I'll go tell Ma she can come back home when she feels like moving." He put a hand on Josiah's shoulder. "Thanks for everything you've done for my family. But right now, you need to pay attention to your father and"—he offered a slow grin—"my sister, if I'm not mistaken." He pushed Josiah in the direction of the cabin. "Go, take care of business, friend."

Josiah strode to the cabin with the lightest heart he had felt in months.

ૐ

A shaft of light told Sally someone had opened the door to the cabin. She felt Josiah's welcome presence before she saw him, and smiled as she turned around to greet him. "He's resting comfortably."

"They're taking Hawkins and the others to gaol as prisoners of war. They'll turn them over to the army as soon as they can figure out how to get them there."

Sally shivered. "Good. Hawkins at least meant serious harm."

"So did my father." Josiah sat next to her and reached for her hand. "How can you be so kind to him, after what he did to you and your family?"

Sally looked at the sleeping figure on the bed. Josiah resembled him so strongly that it was like looking at a portrait of him from the future. "He's your father. How can I do any less?"

"Oh, Sally." Josiah lifted her hand to his lips and kissed her fingertips. "I don't deserve you."

A pleasant shiver ran through Sally's body, a portend of better times ahead. Ma had given birth to a healthy baby boy, the confrontation between the Patriots and Tories had ended without bloodshed, and their harvest was safe. So far, Mr. Tuttle had survived. "God is so good. He has been a strong habitation on this day."

"Amen." Josiah smiled. "The doctor left some medicines for Father with us."

"Go get them." Sally didn't hesitate. "He is resting now, but

I don't know what to expect when he awakens."

Josiah kissed her fingers again and left. The door closed behind him.

"Hah!" Mr. Tuttle opened his eyes at the noise. "Josiah?" The words came out faint.

"He's gone for your medicine. He'll be back as soon as he can."

"Sally Reid." Mr. Tuttle said each syllable slowly, painfully, before slipping back into unconsciousness.

Sally didn't know whether he said her name as a question or a curse. It didn't matter. He was Josiah's father, and she would love him and care for him as if he were her own dear pa come back to life.

&

Peace at last. Sally valued these quiet hours when the men went to the fields to harvest the crops. Most days they allowed Nellie to tag along. After the close quarters in the cave, the cabin seemed spacious indeed. Even so, the family made a fair amount of noise before they headed out to the fields before daybreak.

Ma left the beans simmering in the kettle and sat down next to the bed where Mr. Tuttle slept. Donny rustled in his cradle, whimpered, and she snuggled him close. "There, there. Ma's got you, and you're safe. Keep quiet so Mr. Tuttle can sleep."

Sally didn't know how Ma did it. Within days of giving birth, she had organized the family's move back to the cabin. She shared housekeeping duties with Sally so that she could sit with Mr. Tuttle. The only thing that kept Ma from going to the fields was the rest of the family's insistence that she take things easy.

"Do you think he's getting better?" Sally asked. She knew so little about apoplexy; she was following the doctor's written directions from last year, praying, and answering when Mr. Tuttle spoke. The most physically demanding part of his care was changing the bedding when the laxative of sweet butter and salt the doctor had recommended did its work. Feeding him his meals of broth, tea, and toast was no trouble at all.

"He still lives. God has shown His great mercy. Josiah has suffered enough." Ma pursed her lips. "More than that, Mr. Tuttle would do well to get out of bed. Perhaps between us, we can help him to his feet the next time he awakens."

Sally hated to ask Ma for help. The baby awakened her at all hours of the day and night. But she couldn't support Mr. Tuttle's weight on her own.

"We'll try."

As if he heard them, Mr. Tuttle stirred, squinting at the sunshine coming through the window. "What day is it?"

That was new. He had been asking where he was upon awakening. Perhaps he was regaining his memory. "It's Friday, Mr. Tuttle."

He raised himself on his elbows and looked around the cabin, sparse since they hadn't yet returned all of their possessions from the cave. "How long. . ." The question tailed off.

"It's been four days since you had an apoplectic fit. Josiah is out with our family, bringing in our harvest and yours, too. He'll be here in the evening."

"That son of mine." The tone hovered between rancor and admiration.

Ma burped Donny and set him back in the cradle. She nodded at Sally, who squared her shoulders.

"Mr. Tuttle, we're going to help you get to your feet."

"Don't need your help." He swung his legs over the side of the bed, panting from the exertion.

"You've been very ill and need to get your strength back. Lean on us, and you can rise." Sally bent over and slipped his arm around her shoulders. Ma did the same thing on his other side and helped him up. He swayed on his feet, his teeth gritted in grim determination.

"Can you walk as far as that chair?" Ma nodded at the seat she had just vacated.

He grunted assent, and they kept pace with him. One step, two brought him to the chair. He sank down in relief.

"It's *so* good to see you up!" Sally wanted to laugh with happiness. Josiah's father was on the mend. "Let me fix you some broth." She dished soup from the kettle where they kept it warm and brought it to him.

When she turned around, he was staring at the baby. "Boy or girl?" he asked.

"A boy. Donald Reid Jr.," Ma said.

"I am sorry for your loss." For the first time since the tragedy at Fort Ticonderoga, he offered condolences.

"As we are for yours. No one can replace a son."

"Nor a spouse. I miss my Martha, away in Canada, but I hope to see her again." He looked sad, and Sally hastened to cheer him.

"Come now and eat. You need to build up your strength." By the time he finished eating, he had tired, and they helped him back into bed.

"Keep up the good work, and soon you'll be able to greet Josiah at the door when he comes back at night." Sally checked his coverings.

"I'd like that."

ð

Every one of Josiah's muscles ached after a stretch of sixteen-hour days. They only rested on the Lord's Day, when work ceased and they worshipped in the cabin. With Nathaniel and Stephen's help, they had brought in all the crops from both farms. God had blessed them with enough to see them through the winter and to share with the Patriot families not as fortunate as they had been in raising crops during these troubled times.

Stephen and Nellie lugged a bucket of corncobs between them for an evening feast. Chewing and swallowing still caused Father problems, but he could eat the kernels if they cut them from the cob. Or Sally might make mush with the fresh grain. Father must be tired of soups and broths. Josiah wanted him to enjoy the plenty with the rest of them.

When they returned to the clearing, Nathaniel headed for the barn to milk the cows while Josiah and Stephen went to the cabin. A smile spread across his face at the thought of seeing Sally. Through the long days of Father's illness, she had been so sweet and hardworking and kind.

The door opened, and instead of Sally, he saw. . .

"Father!"

Clinging to a cane, his father stood straight and proud.

Josiah rushed forward and embraced him. "It's good to see you on your feet and walking, sir!"

Sally had assured Josiah that his father was making progress, but he'd had little opportunity to observe with the long hours of work. Once or twice, Father had been sitting in a chair, finishing his meal, when they returned. An unspoken truce existed between them, and they had exchanged little beyond pleasantries.

"I've received excellent care." Father gestured at Sally and Mrs. Reid as if they were friends and allies. Never had his father's words sounded so sweet to Josiah's ears.

Father wobbled, and Sally took his arm. "Don't press too close. And now"—she smiled up at Father—"you promised to sit back down."

"I did, didn't I?" He turned around good-humoredly and accepted Sally's assistance to sit in his usual chair. "There. I've done as I promised. Now let me have a few minutes alone with my son."

She smiled indulgently at him. "We'll leave you two alone for a few moments while we shuck the corn. Don't take too long."

Mrs. Reid had already joined the others outside. Both Father and Josiah stared after Sally's departing back. When she closed the door, Father cleared his throat.

"Son, I have some things I need to talk with you about. Last year, the doctor warned me not to get too riled up or something even worse might happen. He was right, and I'm not only talking about this." He gestured to his body.

"Father, you're still recovering. This may not be a good time to talk." Josiah didn't know if he wanted to delay this conversation more for his sake or for his father's.

"This won't take long." Father paused to take a deep breath. "I've been every kind of fool. I still believe the Bible commands us to honor the king, but I've had no right to treat you as I have. To blame you for Solomon's death. The Lord gives and the Lord takes away. Not me, not the king, not the Patriots—not you. Can you ever forgive me?"

Even more convincing than Father's words were the tears in his eyes. The hard, cold, hurt place that had resided in

Josiah's breast since Solomon's death broke apart. "Can you forgive me for taking him with me into danger?"

"There is nothing to forgive." Father reached up his arms, rather like a child asking for his mother, and Josiah embraced him. When he felt the older man tremble, he released him.

"Let me get—"

"Wait a moment. I have one more thing I need to say." Father's voice was sharp. "You'll be ten times the fool I've been if you let a woman like Sally get away. You two belong together. Mr. Reid knew it, and I knew it until I let pride and anger get in the way."

Josiah felt tears in his own eyes. "So we have your blessing?"

"You have my blessing."

Josiah shouted so loud that the entire Reid family barged in.

epilogue

"Ma says you'd best hurry up. If you stay in that water much longer, you'll be all wrinkled for your wedding." Nellie peeked around the curtain. "Are you almost done?"

"I'm coming." Sally sighed and reached for the towel Ma had set aside for her use. She felt clean, inside and out, and couldn't wait for the morrow, when she would wed Josiah Tuttle.

To think that only a few weeks ago she had thought this day would never come. After Mr. Tuttle gave his blessing to the couple, Josiah had once again asked her to marry him. This time she'd said yes.

Since Nathaniel and Stephen had been banished to the barn while the ladies prepared for Sally's big day, she slipped on a robe and sat before the fire. Ma took out her beautiful, mother-of-pearl comb she saved for special occasions and worked on Sally's hair.

"I know I gave my blessing for you to marry Josiah, but I didn't expect such short notice." Ma sounded aggrieved and then softened her tone. "You're my firstborn, and it's hard to let go."

"We couldn't know a circuit rider would come into town before Josiah had to leave. He and Nathaniel are itching to join the Green Mountain Boys."

"And you may not see him again for months. I remember what it's like to be young and in love." Ma's hands tugged at a knot in Sally's hair. She made a small sound, and baby Donny responded with a whimper. They both looked at the infant.

Ma spoke again. "Of course you want that time together, and maybe even, with God's blessing, a living reminder of your union." She hugged her daughter. "I pray he comes back to you safe and sound."

Sally's heart tensed. Josiah faced a difficult road. First he would escort his father to Canada, where he could wait with his wife and others loyal to the king until the war ended. If he remained in Maple Notch after he recovered from his illness, Mr. Tuttle faced the same prison sentence the other Tories had received. After that, Josiah would join the Green Mountain Boys and fight for freedom.

Between now and then, they would have one blessed day and night.

Sally planned to enjoy every minute of their time together.

❧

The following morning, Josiah woke earlier than usual. How good God was. The necessity of leaving Maple Notch before he could wed Sally had pained Josiah, yet his father's safety and the call of the militia had to come first. But then the circuit rider had appeared in town on Sunday and agreed to wed them. They would have a day and night together before his departure, time they would spend in the cave that had sheltered the Reid family over the summer.

"I've got your razor ready for you." Father had set out essentials for grooming. "And something else." He shook out a velvet jacket in the old style, a trifle worn but elegant and well made. "I wore this when I married your mother. You haven't had time to get new clothes made, nor even to wash the ones you have. I'd consider it an honor if you would wear this. We're much of a size. It should fit."

Josiah had considered himself fortunate that his best breeches were clean. Now he had a gentleman's coat to wear with his cleanest shirt. "I only hope Sally will be as fortunate."

Father chuckled. "If I know Mary Reid, she has something up her sleeve for the girl." He held up the coat for Josiah to put it on. "Besides, you wouldn't care if she wore her milking dress. Come, let's get going."

❧

Everyone left in town gathered under the sugar maples, elms, and oaks that sheltered the green, their bright autumn colors carpeting the ground underfoot. Cold snapped in the air, a hint of the coming winter days. Sally's thoughts strayed to the layers of petticoats that served to keep her warm.

The preacher stood in the center of the green, but she scarcely noticed him. Josiah waited, resplendent in a soft blue coat and white shirt, dark hair pulled back with a plain black ribbon. She gripped the basket of asters Nellie had gathered and walked toward the altar.

Toward the future.

Toward freedom.

Together.

A Letter To Our Readers

Dear Reader:

In order that we might better contribute to your reading enjoyment, we would appreciate your taking a few minutes to respond to the following questions. We welcome your comments and read each form and letter we receive. When completed, please return to the following:

Fiction Editor
Heartsong Presents
PO Box 719
Uhrichsville, Ohio 44683

1. Did you enjoy reading *The Prodigal Patriot* by Darlene Franklin?
   ❏ Very much! I would like to see more books by this author!
   ❏ Moderately. I would have enjoyed it more if

   _____

   _____

   _____

2. Are you a member of **Heartsong Presents**? ❏ Yes ❏ No
   If no, where did you purchase this book? _____

   _____

3. How would you rate, on a scale from 1 (poor) to 5 (superior), the cover design? _____

4. On a scale from 1 (poor) to 10 (superior), please rate the following elements.

   ____ Heroine   ____ Plot
   ____ Hero   ____ Inspirational theme
   ____ Setting   ____ Secondary characters

5. These characters were special because? _____

_____

_____

6. How has this book inspired your life? _____

_____

_____

7. What settings would you like to see covered in future
   Heartsong Presents books? _____

_____

_____

8. What are some inspirational themes you would like to see
   treated in future books? _____

_____

_____

9. Would you be interested in reading other **Heartsong
   Presents** titles? ❑ Yes ❑ No

10. Please check your age range:
     ❑ Under 18   ❑ 18-24
     ❑ 25-34   ❑ 35-45
     ❑ 46-55   ❑ Over 55

Name _____

Occupation _____

Address _____

City, State, Zip _____

E-mail _____

THE GUNSMITH'S GALLANTRY

Shy gunsmith Hiram Dooley has woman troubles. His sister's about to leave him to marry his best friend; his sister-in-law feels it's his duty to marry her since they're both widowed; and the woman he really loves, Libby Adams, has no idea of his esteem—and he isn't sure how to tell her.

Historical, paperback, 320 pages, 5³⁄₁₆" x 8"

_____

Heart♥ong

Presents

Great Inspirational Romance at a Great Price!

Heartsong Presents books are inspirational romances in contemporary and historical settings, designed to give you an enjoyable, spirit-lifting reading experience. You can choose wonderfully written titles from some of today's best authors like Wanda E. Brunstetter, Mary Connealy, Susan Page Davis, Cathy Marie Hake, Joyce Livingston, and many others.

When ordering quantities less than twelve, above titles are $2.97 each.
Not all titles may be available at time of order.